Es'kia Mphahlele

Renewal Time

readers international

Published by Readers International Inc., USA, and Readers
International, London. Editorial inquiries to London office at
8 Strathray Gardens, London NW3 4NY, England. US/Canadian
inquiries to Subscriber Service Department, P.O. Box 959,
Columbia, Louisiana 71418-0959 USA.

Cover Art: *Columned*, painting by Ablade Glover, Ghana,
courtesy of the October Gallery, London.
Cover design by Jan Brychta
Typesetting by Opus 43, Cumbria UK
Printed and bound in Great Britain by Richard Clay Ltd,
Bungay, Suffolk

Library of Congress Catalog Card Number: 88-61391

British Library Cataloguing in Publication Data
Mphahlele, Es'kia
Renewal Time: stories.
I. Title
823 [F]

ISBN 0-930523-55-5 Hardcover
ISBN 0-930523-56-3 Paperback

Contents

"The Sounds Begin Again" forms the opening chapter of *Afrika My Music* (1984), the author's autobiography of his exile years and his return to South Africa.

The Sounds Begin Again

I am sitting out on the stoep of our house at Lebowa-kgomo, fifty kilometres south-east of Pietersburg. A city in the making. In front of our row is bush. Pitch dark. Not more than six kilometres to the north, beyond the bush through which the Tudumo river cuts, is the hill. A narrow valley away from the hill is the Mogodumo mountain range. Further on, out of my line of vision, Mogodumo is severed at Chuene's Pass for the road that runs from Lydenburg to Pietersburg. Mogodumo-tona (masculine in Sesotho) is the huge, imposing part of the range to the left of Chuene's Pass. The part in front of us is Mogodumo-tshadi (feminine). Partly because the name itself suggests a superhuman rumbling within that sheer bulk of rock heaving against space, I like to think of Mogodumo as the mountain of the gods.

Twelve kilometres to the east is Maupaneng, the village in the Mphahlele district where I spent seven years of my childhood, looking after cattle and goats. The mountain dark and its boulder-heaving rivers has since those days held some enchantment for me. In all the years of our exile we did not encounter such a river as the Hlakaro is on its journey through Maupaneng. Apart from the Congo in parts, and the Zambezi at the famous falls, the rivers have been placid, heavy-bosomed.

Every so often I jog in the Mphahlele district and trace the goat-and-cattle trails we maintained in my herdboy days. I still remember them vividly. On these excursions I try to recapture the smells of the place. So often I am jolted out of my reverie by the birdsong of my youth. I pick up *morula* fruit and berries, and the taste travels back forty-seven years. I left these haunts in 1930 and did not return until July 1976.

Pitch darkness, riotous moonlight, night sounds, boulder-heaving rivers, orchestrated by stories about giants and huge snakes before which man humbled himself — all these filled my life as a boy with terror. Now I drive home from Pietersburg in the moonlight, and approach the moon-blanched length of rock on the feminine side of Chuene's Pass. Suddenly I am startled by the overhanging shadow of the male on my right. I can't help feeling the protective embrace of the silence as I make my passage, the male and female reaching out towards each other through moonlight and shadows.

Philadelphia, Pennsylvania, is a long way off now. In the months since our arrival on August 17, 1977, it has become a sporadic memory. We shipped back all we owned, but the real investment required of us was the emotional and spiritual energy it took to accomplish this return from twenty years of exile. Problems of re-entry, political decisions and psychological readjustments have simply pushed America into some corner of the mind.

For four full months I waited for a reply from the University of the North, Sovenga. I could not see why I should not be given the professorship of English, and yet I was apprehensive. So was Rebecca. They gave me the run-around for it, too. There was an interview at Pretoria University, after which I was advised to meet the Personnel Officer at Sovenga to discuss conditions of service. I might well have had the feeling that I was in — the only candidate to come up for an interview, they said.

The reply came. Curt and cold: "Your application has been unsuccessful . . ." The official crap and all. The muck and the smell of it . . . I felt bitter. The South African Consulate in Washington D.C. had read out to me a letter from the Department of the Interior stating that I would be allowed to return to South Africa, on condition that I came to reside in Lebowa and sought employment at the University of the North. To get that far had required a five-year negotiation with the government through the good offices of the Chief Minister of Lebowa, Dr C.C. Phatudi. I could taste gall in my mouth . . .

Before we left South Africa in September, 1957, to teach in Nigeria, I used to sit on the stoep of my house in Orlando West, Soweto. I looked out towards the lights of white suburbia, Northcliff especially, across the darkness. Lights that always enchanted me. I was waiting for my passport, waiting for the exit gates to open. After fifteen months of harrowing speculation attended by doubts and fore-bodings, the passport came, a day before my departure.

This time, in 1977, I was waiting for the inner gates to be opened. After twenty years in the international community, where merit counts most in my line of work — where, after my application for the first Nigerian job, I had always been *invited* to academic positions — I had returned to a country where the black man has learned to wait, endure, survive.

I was indeed back home.

Tonight, a week before 1979 breaks upon us, as we sit out on this stoep in Lebowakgomo a few kilometres from Capricorn, Rebecca and I feel our optimism has been partly vindicated. The University of the Witwatersrand has offered me a position in its African Studies Institute as Senior Research Fellow. I have accepted, and shall begin on the first day of February. Also, the Minister of Justice has taken my name off the list of those writers who may not be quoted, whose works may not circulate in the country. Back in April 1966, I was one of a whole batch of writers living abroad who were "listed" under the Internal Security Act. Only *Down Second Avenue, Voices in the Whirlwind*, and *Modern African Stories*, which I co-edited, may now be read in the country. *The African Image* (revised edition), *In Corner B and Other Stories* and *The Wanderers* remain banned under the Publications and Entertainment Act. The Vice-Chancellor of the University of the Witwatersrand and the lawyer, Ismail Ayob, had simultaneously petitioned the then Minister of Justice to remove me from the list of the gagged, otherwise I would not even be able to circulate my notes in class.

After my reversal at Sovenga, Rebecca took up a job as community social worker under the Lebowa Government Service. She has a Master's degree in Social Work from the University of Denver. I was employed by Lebowa's Department of Education as inspector in charge of English teaching.

During ten months travelling the length and breadth of Lebowa, I discovered what twenty-five years of Bantu

Education have done to the standard of English. Just flattened it. Not that white students entering university are much better equipped, though this is for different reasons. Among Africans there was greater competence in the use of English before 1958 — among both teachers and pupils. Progressively fewer students have been majoring in English, still fewer proceeding to the Honours degree.

These tours of duty gave me perspective; they made me long for the classroom. To make it worse, Lebowa, like other territories that are supposed to be managing their own education departments, does not have the money for a full-scale attempt to upgrade teachers and training institutions. The system is still "Bantu Education". Its key functionaries are whites seconded by the central government who enjoy extra pay for "hazards" or "hardships" because they are supposed to be working in outpost conditions.

The English-language press championed my cause when I lost the Sovenga post. Government officials refused to answer their questions. The university administration, Rector and all, let it be known that the then Minister of Education and Training had turned down its unanimous decision to appoint me. The Minister refused to give reasons. He promised, though, that he would veto any appointment Ezekiel Mphahlele might be given by any university or other institution under his control. Someone in the university administration came out with it at last: it was not the policy of the central government to let blacks chair departments like English.

I began to understand why the university had not been seen to put pressure on the Minister to take the man they wanted — though they believed, according to their statements in the press, that my academic qualifications were "unimpeachable". What was harder to understand was why they had staged that farcical interview at Pretoria University in the first place.

The interview! The atmosphere is weird. The Registrar — a Mr Steenkamp — gives me a curt nod as I enter the room, and motions me to my seat. The committee consists of the Rector of the University of the North (the late Dr Kgware); Professor Leighton, head of English at the Rand Afrikaans University; Professor Sebaga, head of English at Pretoria University; Professor Mativha, head of Venda at the University of the North; and Professor Pretorius, head of History at the same place.

Only the men from Pretoria and the Rand ask academic and pedagogic questions. The African professor restricts himself to one question, which does not give rise to discussion: do I think African languages are important enough for us to continue to teach them?

The Rector asks what I understand by university autonomy and academic freedom in relation to the University of the North. Dr History asks why I have come back to seek employment in an institution that is a product of the system of education I had attacked before I left the country? Why have I come back to a country whose whites are racist as I describe them in the subtitle of a poem of mine? What position would I take if the students rioted?

We tell whites a million lies a day in this country. First, because we must survive, second, because they themselves already live a big lie. Lying to the white man who employed me or who processed my life was a natural thing to do before I left South Africa. I learned to be relatively at ease with whites abroad, and I did not have to lie in order to survive. I could sell my labour on the best market. In the process I either unlearned or tucked away in some corner of the subconscious the impulse to tell a white man lies. It is no effort for me to tell the appointments committee in front of me the truth about my views on the matters raised.

It is only after I have left the Senate room that it occurs to me that I have repeatedly talked about the "independent states north of the Limpopo river" to distinguish them from South Africa. Academic freedom and university autonomy? A university should be accorded the universal right to develop its own curricula in a way that reflects the culture in which it is operating, and in turn feed something into that culture so that it does not stagnate. An African university must express African culture even if white expatriates still teach in it. I should like to think also that a South African university will feel constrained to work towards a future that will make the concept of "separate development" irrelevant; that curricula and syllabuses can express a culture striving towards a synthesis that will be truly *African*.

An African university should be manned by the people best equipped, in the context of today's separateness, to perceive and promote the black man's aspirations. As soon as possible we should employ an increasing number of Africans. But Africanization should not mean merely employing more African teachers; curricula and syllabuses should increasingly be Africa-based, instead of constantly singing the triumphs of Western civilization. For instance, African literature should be the starting point from which we can fan outwards. The English department should become a department of literature, an integral part of which would be comparative literary studies. And the more obvious principles: a university should promote freedom of inquiry, freedom of speech.

I cannot help but read mischief in Dr History's question about my return. It seems to suggest that I am unique. I merely answer: I wanted to return to my ancestral home — South Africa; I want a meaningful cultural context to work in; I want community. I left the country because I was banned from teaching; I did not skip the country nor leave on an exit permit. If I had continued to teach I would still have opposed Bantu Education. Who loves everything the government of his country does? My return has ultimately got nothing to do with whether I like the system or not. I have always believed that the democratic ideal should accommodate political dissent. How about that, Dr History?

Students rioting? I would not encourage it. But after saying this, I should point out that students want a representative council (I have heard of one that was banned at Sovenga) that can be respected and accommodated by the administration. Candid debate must be allowed for and listened to seriously. How about that, Dr History?

As a parting shot, Dr History asks how members of the Congress for Cultural Freedom will view my return to a country they have repeatedly condemned. I answer that I had not thought it necessary to institute a referendum on whether or not I should return.

Booby traps, booby traps . . . Intellectual integrity, where is your home, where is your sanctuary? I later learned that stock questions about academic freedom and university autonomy were part of the repertoire on these occasions.

A white man from the University of South Africa was appointed. If God moves like a crab, as we say in our languages, what simile would be fitting for the way the South African government works? After this, I was invited by heads of departments at two other "ethnic" universities to consider the possibility of joining their departments. I was agreeable. Somewhere along the line internal negotiations struck bedrock. Some top university official teetered on the edge of the cliff and then turned round to tell my promoters that he was afraid the government would not approve . . . We often fail to see the strings by which the bantustan puppet moves in the floodlights, but the full-bodied dancer — how can *that* escape us?

I stop to contemplate a serenity I have rediscovered in the northern Transvaal landscape. I realize how cosmopolitan, how suburban my family's lifestyle has become; for better, for worse, we have become bigger than our urban ghetto beginnings. The bonds that have held us to the original African experience, though, have remained intact during our travels. We still feel a strong identity with our ancestors: the living dead who are the spiritual dimension of our reason for returning. *Come back native son, native daughter come back!*

In the last year I have been reacquainting myself with the smell and texture of the place. A changed human landscape in many ways, one that is still changing but essentially still real to me. Pockets of African urban life have broken into the idyllic rural scene. Boys no longer herd cattle and goats: instead, they go to school regularly. Women still carry water on their heads for long distances, either from a river or from a communal pump. Just as they used to fifty years ago when I was a boy and, of course, for centuries before. Field husbandry has diminished considerably owing to the disruptive impact of the migrant-labour system and the lack of good land. Those who come back to live here go in for small-scale commercial ventures or into professional and administrative jobs. What else could there be in the midst of all this rural poverty?

Yes, a changing human landscape, but still essentially rural, though now Mirage aircraft from the military bases further north come whizzing and piercing through space overhead every so often. From the southern urban complex, echoes of another turbulence and pain come to my ears like the sound of ocean breakers staking a claim on the shore. The imagination is straining for the meaning of this confluence: super-tensed birds of steel from the north, the painful south and its turbulence down there, and between them, this pastoral serenity and I, who have in the last twenty years become thoroughly suburban. So much so that, because I could live anywhere I liked abroad if I could afford it, I wonder now that I am back home what slum living would be like.

A poem is straining to be born. It was Vinoba Bhave, the Indian mystic, who said: "Though action rages without, the heart can be tuned to produce unbroken music . . ." Super-tensed jets, political noises, the power drills of the south and their tremors, the wanderer returned to look for physical, and a social and cultural commitment . . . My very return is a compromise between the outsider who did not *have* to be bullied by place in other lands (and yet wanted a place, badly) and the insider who has an irrepressible attachment to ancestral place, be it in a rural or an urban setting.

Like the rest, I must submit to the pull of place, I must deal with the tyranny of time. This composition — the border between us and Zimbabwe, Mozambique and other territories, the birds of steel seeming to spoil for a fight, this serenity, the turbulent south — let it strain at our hearts; if our hearts be found whole, we are content.

During those highly impressionable years as a herdboy in the Mphahlele district, I got to know fear. Fear of the dark, fear of high mountains in which I had to spend hours looking for lost cattle or hunting rabbits. Fear of rivers that tumbled down, uprooting trees and boulders. I got to know the cruelties and benignities of nature. Then I became an urban dweller in Pretoria, where I had been born. I came to love it, in that mindless way a child can be said to love a place, with all its filth, odours, terrors, poverty, death. Because of the memory of those years, when we seemed to grow up casually, when we were always liable to be crushed by the life Pretoria and Cape Town had planned for us, I cannot today help feeling nostalgic about the sense of community we shared in Marabastad; nostalgic even about the smells, the taste and the texture of life as we experienced it in those days — even though I would not want to live in a slum again. Never. Those terrors of rural and urban life became rooted in me so that I could never, even in my adult life, outgrow them. They haunt my dreams today, they help define my responses to life wherever I live it, among other humans and in my books.

Some African poets, particularly the Francophone poets, have sweet things to say about night. Night as a symbol of blackness. Night "teeming with rainbows" as Aimé Césaire would say. Night of ourselves. Black souls communing with night and listening to its mysteries, night defining black souls and their pride. Night was no longer to represent the ugly, the mysterious, the sinister, the darkness of spirit. After the terrors of pastoral life, *my* nights in the slum were orchestrated only by screams, moans, police whistles, the screech of squad car tyres. Life became a myriad burning fuses, each radiating its own dump of explosives. Explosives that seem to renew themselves by their own rubble and ashes, creating always their own fuses in the process. In our African townships we seek the day, not the night.

The tyranny of time, the tyranny of place . . . The muck, the smell of it, the fever and the fight, the cycles of decay and survival . . . And "the sounds begin again". I want daytime, I want place, I want a sense of history. Even though place will never be the same again for me, because its lights and shadows may change, I want to be there when it happens.

The tyranny of time, the tyranny of place . . . The muck and smell of it . . . Back to 1941 when, at twenty-one, I took up my first job as a teacher of the blind in an adult institution, Roodepoort. Fresh from teacher training, from the protection of boarding-school life, utterly confused. I made up my mind to finish high school by private study and proceed by the same route up to the M.A. I lived in another slum fifty miles from my place of birth, and it could have been that Pretoria slum transplanted. Night screams, barking of half-starved mongrels, the rattle of wagons loaded with human manure collected from lavatory buckets . . . the smell of night . . . the throb of a life seeking at once some violent release, some affectionate contact and a corner to deal with the terrors of night, to take stock of the hurts, the buffetings, the braveries of daytime . . .

Something strange happened to me as I studied by candlelight, listening at intervals to the throb of night out there. I found myself writing a short story. During my primary school days, I had rooted everywhere for newsprint to read. Any old scrap of paper. Our ghetto had no newspaper deliveries, no school libraries (forty years later we still don't have them) . . . There was a small one-room tin shack the municipality had the sense of humour to call a "reading room", on the western edge of Marabastad. It was stacked with dilapidated books and journals junked by some bored ladies in the suburbs. Anything from cookery books through boys' and girls' adventure to dream interpretation and astrology. Needless to say, mostly useless. But I dug out of the pile Cervantes' *Don Quixote*. I went through the whole lot like a termite, elated by the sense of discovery, of recognition of the printed word, by mere practice of the skill of reading. But Cervantes was to stand out in my mind, forever.

Another thing that fired my imagination was the silent movies of the Thirties. Put Don Quixote and Sancho Panza together with Laurel and Hardy, with Harold Lloyd, with Buster Keaton, with all those heroes of American cowboy folklore — Hoot Gibson, Tim McCoy, Buck Jones and so on. Put Don Quixote next to Tarzan the Ape or Tarzan the Tiger: a crazy world. And yet unwittingly we wanted just this kind of entertainment to help us cope with the muck and the smell and the demands for gut response of every-day life. As I read the subtitles aloud to my friends who could not read as fast or at all, amid the yells and foot stamping and bouncing on chairs to the rhythm of the action, amid the fierce clanking of the piano near the stage of the movie house — as I did all this, fantastical ideas were whipping around in my mind. I was intrigued, captivated by the age-old technique of story-telling. All we saw in the movies, all we read in those journals and books, was about faraway lands, not our own sordid setting. It was an exciting release, although we were mindless of the reasons for it.

I recount all this to indicate some of the equipment I brought to the adventure I found myself embarked upon before I knew it. I had not read any short stories before — of the artful kind we compose today. Lots of tales, yes. So I had no genuine models. I simply stacked them up without any hope of publishing what I wrote, as it would have been unthinkable for a white magazine even to consider them; or even a white-owned newspaper circulating among Africans. Looking back on the stories now, they read hopelessly like the kind of thing that aspires to be a novel and so fails to make the incisive point it set out to, capturing only the aura of tragedy that surrounds black life. I wrote simply to depict the situation and the human beings who act it out, without the technique by which dramatic and rhetorical connections are made between real-life suffering, the socio-political system, and art. My focus was always the drama of life as lived in the ghetto. I saw "white" life merely as peripheral. The exercise in literary compromise had begun for me, something even more profound than what is often referred to as "writing yourself out of a situation". And the sounds begin again . . . Outside there, from inside this tin shack in Roodepoort location, I can hear a wedding song. The singers will stop at our corner, I'm sure, to dance. The moon is out. Its light will be trying to bounce off the corrugated-iron roofs, but rust will resist that moongame. Maybe I'll step out for a little diversion when the group comes round the corner.

Four and a half years later, I had finished my high-school course and was eligible for high school teaching. But I would have to continue with private study. I went to Orlando, 1945. And the sounds begin again . . . the gang wars, the police squad cars, the political rallies, the baton charges, cops shooting . . . high-school teaching and further self-education. A new phase for me: teaching English in a ghetto. Every teacher in my schooldays had tried blissfully and unwittingly to murder any love I had for literature. Walter Scott, Jane Austen, Dryden, Milton, Richard Steele, Joseph Addison, Thackeray — imagine this forbidding line-up in an African setting! Throughout my junior high school days, let alone before that, through the Forties, mission schools allowed no one to teach English who was not of English stock. We had to pass exams; we had to succeed. Our parents had little or no education themselves: we had been told education was the key to a decent livelihood and respectability, and we wanted those — oh, how desperately we wanted them in order to rise spiritually above our sordid conditions. So we had to chew on a lot of literary sawdust and wash it down with a smile. I had thus come out of that bludgeoning with perhaps a fragment of Dickens, a chunk of undigested Shakespeare. I resisted Milton until I ceased to care which paradise was lost, which was regained. How can I even now engage our African students in the epic sweep of that poetry when I myself do not identify with a lost paradise? Man's first disobedience — that can be a mighty big joke in Africa. Yet we keep swallowing the Hebrew myths and folklore, and their poetry escapes us. But we had to be subjected to that theology, just as we had been baptized while our infant eyes were barely open, with no say in the matter but a yell in the minister's face. Hence the name Ezekiel or Es'kia: heavy stuff, man, heavy . . .

I rediscovered Dickens, the classics. I discovered Gorky, Dostoevsky, Chekhov, in my private studies and preparations for my classes. Somewhere along the line, my high school students and I discovered each other. I was constantly asking myself questions relating to the value of poetry for me and my students, and for the township culture we were sharing — a culture that was very much an assertion of the human spirit fighting for survival against forces that threatened to fragment or break it. Of what use was poetry in a social climate that generated so much physical violence? In a life that resisted any individual creative efforts, a social climate that made the study of literature, particularly in a foreign but official language like English, look like playing a harmonica or jew's-harp in the midst of sirens and power drills and fire-brigade bells? It was the full recognition of these factors by students and teacher that conditioned the love we developed for literature. A love that had to be self-generated, given all the hostile external factors. The element of escapism also helped sustain that interest. Just as Cervantes, Laurel and Hardy, Buck Jones had served us when I was a boy. An element of escapism that one would have been ashamed in later years to acknowledge, because a few steps from there could land you in sheer snobbery. And snobbery is the cruellest joke anyone can play on himself in an African township. For me, as one who was then writing short stories, the whole literary adventure was a compromise between several disparate drives and urges.

Underlying the questions that we grappled with about the function of literature was always the motivation to master English at the grassroots level of practical usage. English, which was not our mother tongue, gave us power, power to master the external world which came to us through it: the movies, household furniture and other domestic equipment, styles of dress and cuisine, advertising, printed forms that regulated some of the mechanics of living and dying, and so on. It was the key to job opportunities in that part of the private sector of industry where white labour unions had little to lose if they let us in.

We had embarked on an adventure. This sense of adventure explains the enthusiasm, the energy, the drive with which Africa all over confronts the imperatives of learning.

It was during this period of self-education, of teaching, trying to understand what my students wanted, that I made three discoveries, all interrelated. Things that were to change my whole outlook, my whole stance, and consequently my literary style. I became sharply aware of the realism of Dickens, Gorky, Chekhov, Hemingway, Faulkner. I became aware of the incisive qualities of the Scottish and English ballads and saw in them an exciting affinity with the way in which the short story works: the single situation rather than a developmental series of events; concentration of the present moment or circumstance; action, vivid and dramatic; singleness and intensity of emotion, generated by the often terrifying and intense focus on a situation: the plotted and episodic nature of the narrative; the way in which character, instead of developing fully, is bounced off; the "telescoping" of where the characters come from and where they are at present; the heightened moment of discovery or illumination; the "leaping and lingering" technique in which the ballad passes from scene to scene in the narrative without having to fill in gaps, leaping over time and space and lingering on those scenes that are colourful and dramatic; the resonances. I have never, since, ceased to be moved by those ballads. They are so close to our own folk tales that depict violence and the supernatural. With so much death and violence around us in the ghetto, we seemed to be reliving those old days when life was so insecure, when nature was both kind and cruel, and when whatever force presided over human affairs abandoned us to our own predatory instincts.

Most directly related to my style and point of view was the third discovery, by chance in the late Forties, of Richard Wright's short stories, *Uncle Tom's Children* (1936). He was an Afro-American novelist who died in exile in Paris in 1960. I smelled our own poverty in his Southern setting. The long searing black song of Wright's people sounded like ours. The agony told me how to use the short story as a way of dealing with my anger and indignation. It was the ideal genre. I fed on the fury and poured more and more vitriol into my words until I could almost taste them. I would come back from work, wait for the time my family would be asleep, do my studies, and return to my short-story writing. I would go out on my Orlando porch for a break, and have a clear view of the distant lights of Northcliff, thirty or so kilometres away. More and more they took on a symbolic meaning for me, those lights, because between me and them was the dense dark, so dense you wanted to compare it with soup. Since my return from the rural north as a boy, electric lights had never ceased to enchant me. They reminded me, as they still do, of the unfriendly darknesses and riotous floods of moonlight in the rural north. Seen from a distance, the lights taunted me, ridiculed me, tantalized me, reassured me, set off in me an urge sometimes to possess them, sometimes to spray them with black paint, to eclipse them one way or the other.

In 1954, Langston Hughes and I were introduced by letter. He sent me his collection of stories, *The Ways of White Folks*, and his poetry collection, *The Weary Blues*.

We were to meet several times in Africa and the United States before he died in 1967. Although he did not have the driving diction that was Wright's trademark, in their own gentle and almost unobtrusive manner Langston's short fiction and poetry did things to me. I realized later that I had needed them both — those two antithetical idioms of black American expression, Wright's and Langston's.

The Stories

Introduction
by the Author

He came out of Amanzimtoti in 1940 with a twenty-one-year-old head full of itself, stuck on itself. At twenty-one you feel you're the centre of the universe. You want to take on the world. And yet you're a mere parcel of confusion. There's a mighty heave in your biology. As if to prepare you for the pole-vault event of your life. And you feel the strain and pain of that heave. Because you're black your aspirations, your hopes, have little to do with social realities. The rapid fluctuations between the high and the low make for dizzy spells, so to speak. The high because you strive to shoot for regions clear of the muck and the smell and all the getting-through objectives set for you as a boy. The low because you're hemmed in, because someone fenced you in and then turned round and told you, "It's rough out there among us white folks; could break you if you tried to compete with us; be warned and enjoy your freedom from unequal competition."

Too scared to move into teaching just yet, he ventured into an unexpected world, the world of the blind and the deaf-mutes. Ezenzeleni, Itereleng, Kutlwanong, Roodepoort, Hammanskraal. Secretarial work, social work, a little teaching, driving, the lot. He waded into this world armed only with a feeble lantern — a pre-matric teacher's certificate.

He responded to the mighty heave, to the urge to write verse and then stories. Stories came pouring out of his head. And he wrote. Fun, exhilaration, escape. He responded to the call to say what was in his soul. The desire to create strong beautiful words. For what publisher? None. *The Bantu World*? *Ilanga lase Natal*? Hardly. They wanted only short-short sketches, less verse. *Drum* was still to be born, almost a decade later. But the heat was on. He wrote for its own sake. For some inner freedom and peace, for equilibrium in a ship riding the formidable spill of the high seas right in the eye of a storm.

And so 1946, *Man Must Live*. A small volume brought out as an experiment by the publisher, Julian Rollnick of African Bookman, Cape Town.

More stories later. Joined the black voices of the Fifties coming through *Drum*. Some appeared in *Drum*, others elsewhere. "The Master of Doornvlei", "Dinner at Eight", "Down the Quiet Street", "The Coffee-cart Girl", "The Woman", "The Woman Walks Out", "The Suitcase".

Exile. First stop Lagos, Nigeria. For a long time the South African scene dominates the mind. Holds on tenaciously for fear of being forgotten. "The Living and the Dead", "He and the Cat".

Next stop Paris, France. The fifth year. Two years in France: the first you spend learning the language and ways of the French. You resist involvement. Gay Paris? You wonder. Its night life, maybe. Its boulevards, pleasant to walk on. But you want people. You can't talk with night life, with boulevards, with the arts of another culture. Talking in the sense of communing. You even become sensitive to some crudities and streaks of cruelty in the French others might not observe. You try to accommodate, or be accommodated by, a city so many people say is wonderful. Some people may enjoy the wine only and stick to that. And you? You're eclectic, and that helps. But you don't want to be involved and thus *forget* where you came from. Yet you want people. So you keep busy at work and write in your free time. To insulate yourself.

The Nigerian memory is still fresh. Hence "The Barber of Bariga" and "A Ballad of Oyo". The deep South continues to claim you. Hence "A Point of Identity", "Grieg on a Stolen Piano", "In Corner B" and "Mrs Plum".

The Living and the Dead

Lebona felt the letter burning in his pocket. Since he had picked it up along the railway it had nagged at him no end.

He would read it during his lunch, he thought. Meantime he must continue with his work, which was to pick up rubbish that people continuously threw on the platform and on the railway tracks. Lebona used a piece of wire with a ball of tar stuck on at the end. One didn't need to bend. One only pressed the ball of tar on a piece of paper or any other rubbish, detached it and threw it into a bag hanging from the shoulder.

A number of things crossed Lebona's mind: the man who had died the previous afternoon. Died, just like that. How could a man die like that — like a rat or a mere dog?

The workers' rush was over. Only a few women sat on the benches on the platform. One was following his movements with her eyes. She sat there, so fat, he observed, looking at him. Just like a woman. She just sat and looked at you for no reason: probably because of an idle mind; maybe she was thinking about everything. Still he knew if he were a fly she might look at him all day. But no, not the letter. She mustn't be thinking about it. The letter in his pocket. It wasn't hers — no, it couldn't be; he had picked it up lower down the line; she could say what she liked, but it wasn't her letter.

That man: who would have thought a man could just die as if death were in one's pocket or throat all the time?

Stoffel Visser was angry; angry because he felt foolish. Everything had gone wrong. And right through his university career Stoffel Visser had been taught that things must go right to the last detail.

"Calm yourself, Stoffel."

"Such mistakes shouldn't ever occur."

"Don't preach, for God's sake!"

Doppie Fourie helped himself to more whisky.

"It's all Jackson's fault," Stoffel said. "He goes out yesterday and instead of being here in the evening to prepare supper he doesn't come. This morning he's still not here, still not here, and I can't get my bloody breakfast in time because I've got to do it myself, and you know I *must* have a good breakfast every day. Worse, my clock is out of order, buggered up man, and the bloody Jackson's not here to wake me up. So I oversleep — that's what happens — and after last night's *braaivleis*, you know. It's five o'clock on a Friday morning, and the bastard hasn't turned up yet. How could I be in time to give Rens the document before the Cape Town train left this morning?"

"Now I think of it, Stoffel," said Fourie, "I can't help thinking how serious the whole thing is. Now the Minister can't have the report to think about it before the session begins. What do we do next?"

"There'll still be enough time to post it by express mail."

Doppie Fourie looked grave.

"You don't have to look as if the sky was about to fall,"

he said, rather to himself than to his friend. "Have another whisky."

Stoffel poured one for himself and his friend. "What a good piece of work we did, Doppie!"

"Bloody good. Did you see this?" Fourie held out a newspaper, pointing his trembling finger at a report. The item said that Africans had held a "roaring party" in a suburban house while the white family were out. There had been feasting and music and dancing.

"See, you see now," said Stoffel, unable to contain his emotion. "Just what I told these fellows on the commission. Some of them are so wooden-headed they won't under-stand simple things like kaffirs swarming over our suburbs, living there, gambling there, breeding there, drinking there, and sleeping there with girls. They won't understand, these stupid fools, until the kaffirs enter their houses and boss them about and sleep with white girls. What's to happen to white civilization?"

"Don't make another speech, Stoffel. We've talked about this so long in the commission I'm simply choking with it."

"Look here, Doppie Fourie, *ou kêrel*, you deceive yourself to think I want to hear myself talk."

"I didn't mean that, Stoffel. But of course you have always been very clever. I envy you your brains. You always have a ready answer to a problem. Anyhow I don't promise to be an obedient listener tonight. I just want to drink."

"C'mon, *ou kêrel*, you know you want to listen. If I feel pressed to speak you must listen, like it or not."

Doppie looked up at Stoffel, this frail-looking man with an artist's face and an intellect that seldom rose to the surface. None of our rugby-playing types with their bravado, Doppie thought. Often he hated himself for feeling so inferior. And all through his friend's miniature oration Doppie's face showed a deep hurt.

"Let me tell you this, *rooinekke*," Stoffel said, "you know I'd rather be touring the whole world and meeting people and cultures and perhaps learning some art myself — I know you don't believe a thing I'm saying — instead of rotting in this hole and tolerating numskulls I'm compelled to work with on committees. Doppie, there must be hundreds of our people who'd rather be doing something else they love best. But we're all tied to some bucking bronco and we must like it while we're still here and work ourselves up into a national attitude. And we've to keep talking, man. We haven't much time to waste looking at both sides of the question like these stupids, *ou kêrel*. That's why it doesn't pay any more to pretend we're being just and fair to the kaffir by controlling him. No use even trying to tell him he's going to like living in enclosures."

"Isn't it because we know what the kaffir wants that we must call a halt to his ambitious wants? The danger, as I see it, *ou kêrel*, isn't merely in the kaffir's increasing anger and desperation. It also lies in our tendency as whites to believe that what we tell him is the truth. And this might drive us to sleep one day — a fatal day, I tell you. It's necessary to keep talking, Doppie, so as to keep jolting the whites into a sharp awareness. It's dangerously easy for the public to forget and go to sleep."

Doppie clapped his hands in applause, half-dazed, half-mocking, half-admiring. At such times he never knew what word could sum up Stoffel Visser. A genius? — yes, he must be. And then Stoffel would say things he had so often heard from others. *Ag*, I knew it — just like all of us — ordinarily stubborn behind those deep-set eyes. And thinking so gave

Doppie a measure of comfort. He distrusted complex human beings because they evaded labels. Life would be so much nicer if one could just take a label out of the pocket and tack it on the lapel of a man's coat. Like the one a lady pins on you to show that you've dropped a coin into her collecting box. As a badge of charity.

"We can't talk too much, *ou kêrel*. We haven't said the last word in that report on kaffir servants in the suburbs."

Day and night for three months Stoffel Visser had worked hard for the commission he was secretary of — the Social Affairs Commission of his Christian Protestant Party. The report of the commission was to have been handed to Tollen Rens, their representative in Parliament who, in turn, had to discuss it with a member of the Cabinet. A rigorous remedy was necessary, it was suggested, for what Stoffel had continually impressed on the minds of his cronies as "an ugly situation". He could have chopped his own head off for failing to keep his appointment with Tollen Rens. And all through Jackson's not coming to wake him up and give him the breakfast he was used to enjoying with an unflagging appetite.

"Right, Stoffel, see you tomorrow at the office." Doppie Fourie was leaving. Quite drunk. He rocked on his heels a bit as he made for the door, a vacant smile playing on his lips.

Although the two men had been friends for a long time, Doppie Fourie could never stop himself feeling humiliated after a serious talk with Stoffel. Visser always overwhelmed him, beat him down and trampled on him with his superior intellect. The more he drank in order to blunt the edge of the pain Stoffel unwittingly caused him, the deeper was the hurt Doppie felt whenever they had been talking shop.

Still, if Fourie never had the strength of mind to wrench himself from Stoffel's grip, his friend did all he could to preserve their companionship, if only as an exhaust-pipe for his mental energy.

Stoffel's mind slowly came back to his rooms — to Jackson in particular. He liked Jackson, his cook, who had served him with the devotion of a trained animal and ministered to all his bachelor whims and eating habits for four years. As he lived in a flat, it was not necessary for Jackson to do the cleaning. This was the work of the cleaner hired by Stoffel's landlord.

Jackson had taken his usual Thursday off. He had gone to Shanty Town, where his mother-in-law lived with his two children, in order to fetch them and take them to the zoo. He had promised so many times to take them there. His wife worked in another suburb. She couldn't go with them to the zoo because, she said, she had the children's sewing to finish.

This was the second time that Jackson had not turned up when he was expected after taking a day off. The first time he had returned the following morning, all apologies. Where could the confounded kaffir be, Stoffel wondered. But he was too busy trying to adjust his mood to the new situation to think of the different things that might have happened to Jackson.

Stoffel's mind turned around in circles without ever coming to a fixed point. It was this, that and then everything. His head was ringing with the voices he had heard so many times at recent meetings. Angry voices of residents who were gradually being incensed by speakers like him, frantic voices that demanded that the number of servants in each household should be brought down because it wouldn't do for blacks to run the suburbs from their quarters in European backyards.

But there were also angry voices from other meetings: if you take the servants away, how are they going to travel daily to be at work on time, before we leave for work ourselves? Other voices: who told you there are too many natives in our yards? Then others: we want to keep as many servants as we can afford.

And the voices became angrier and angrier, roaring like a sea in the distance and coming nearer and nearer to shatter his complacency. The voices spoke in different languages, gave different arguments, often using different premises to assert the same principles. They spoke in soft, mild tones and in urgent and hysterical moods.

The mind turned around the basic argument in a turmoil: you shall not, we will; we can, you can't; they shall not, they shall. Why must they? Why mustn't they? Some of these kaffir-lovers, of course, hate the thought of having to forego the fat feudal comfort of having cheap labour within easy reach when we remove black servants to their own locations, Stoffel mused.

And amid these voices he saw himself working and sweating to create a theory to defend ready-made attitudes, stock attitudes that various people had each in their own time planted in him: his mother, his father, his brothers, his friends, his schoolmasters, his university professors and all the others who claimed him as their own. He was fully conscious of the whole process in his mind. Things had to be done with conviction or not at all.

Then, even before he knew it, those voices became an echo of other voices coming down through the centuries: the echo of gunfire, cannon, wagon-wheels as they ground away over stone and sand; the echo of hate and vengeance. All he felt was something in his blood which groped back through the corridors of history to pick up some of the broken threads that linked his life with a terrible past. He surrendered himself to it all, to this violent desire to remain part of a brutal historic past, lest he should be crushed by the brutal necessities of the present, and be forced to lose his identity: Almighty God, no, no! Unconsciously he was trying to pile on layers of crocodile hide over his flesh to protect himself against the thoughts or feelings that might some day in the vague future threaten to hurt.

When he woke from a stupor, Stoffel Visser remembered Jackson's wife over at Greenside. He had not asked her if she knew where his servant was. He jumped up and dialled on his telephone. He called Virginia's employer and asked him. No, Virginia didn't know where her husband was. As far as she knew her husband had told her the previous Sunday that he was going to take the children to the zoo. What could have happened to her husband, she wanted to know. Why hadn't he telephoned the police? Why hadn't he phoned Virginia in the morning? Virginia's master asked him these and several other questions. He got annoyed because he couldn't answer them.

None of the suburban police stations or Marshall Square Station had Jackson's name in their charge books. They would let him know "if anything turned up". A young voice from one police station said perhaps Stoffel's "kaffir" had gone to sleep with his "maid" elsewhere and had forgotten to turn up for work. Or, he suggested, Jackson might be under a hangover in the location. "You know what these kaffirs are." And he laughed with a thin sickly voice. Stoffel banged the receiver down.

There was a light knock at the door of his flat. When he opened it with anticipation he saw an African standing erect, hat in hand.

"Yes?"

"Yes, *Baas.*"

"What do you want?"

"I bring you this, *Baas,*" handing a letter to the white man, while he thought: *just like those white men who work for the railways . . . it's good I sealed it . . .*

"Whose is this? It's addressed here, to Jackson! Where did you find it?"

"I was clean the line, *Baas.* Um pick papers and rubbish on railway line at Park Stish. Um think of something as um work. Then I pick up this. I ask *my*-self, who could have dropped it? But . . ."

"All right, why didn't you take it to your boss?"

"They keep letters there many months, *Baas,* and no one comes for them." His tone suggested that Stoffel should surely know that.

The cheek he has, finding fault with the way the white man does things.

"You lie! You opened it first to see what's inside. When you found no money you sealed it up and were afraid your boss would find out you had opened it. Not true?"

"It's not true, *Baas.* I was going to bring it here whatever happened."

He fixed his eyes on the letter in Stoffel's hand. "Truth's God, *Baas,*" Lebona said, happy to be able to lie to someone who had no way of divining the truth, thinking at the same time: *they're not even decent enough to suspect one's telling the truth!*

They always lie to you when you're white, Stoffel thought, *just for cheek*.

The more Lebona thought he was performing a just duty the more annoyed the white man was becoming.

"Where do you live?"

"Kensington, *Baas*. Um go there now. My wife she working there."

Yet another of them, eh? Going home in a white man's area — we'll put a stop to that yet — and look at the smugness on his mug!

"All right, go." All the time they were standing at the door, Stoffel thought how the black man smelled of sweat, even though he was standing outside.

Lebona made to go and then remembered something. Even before the white man asked him further he went on to relate it all, taking his time, with his emotions spilling over.

"I feel very sore in my heart, *Baas*. This poor man, he comes out of train. There are only two lines of steps on platform, and I say to *my*-self how can people go up when others are coming down? You know, there are iron gates now, and only one go and come at a time. Now other side there's train to leave for Orlando."

What the hell have I to do with this? What does he think this is, a complaints office?

"Now, you see, it's like this: a big crowd go up and a big crowd want to rush for their train. Um look and whistle and says to *my*-self how can people move in different ways like that? Like a river going against another!"

One of these kaffirs who think they're smart, eh.

"This man, I've been watching him go up. I see him

pushed down by those on top of steps. Rush down and stamp on him and kick him. He rolls down until he drops back on platform. Blood comes out mouth and nose like rain and I say to *my*-self, oho he's dead, poor man!"

I wish he didn't keep me standing here listening to a story about a man I don't even care to know! . . .

"The poor man died, just like that, just as if I went down the stairs now and then you hear um dead."

I couldn't care less either. . . .

"As um come here by tram I think, perhaps this is his letter."

"All right now, I'll see about that."

Lebona walked off with a steady and cautious but firm step. Stoffel was greatly relieved.

Immediately he rang the hospital and mortuary, but there was no trace of Jackson. Should he or should he not read the letter? It might give him a clue. But, no, he wasn't a *kaffir*!

Another knock at the door.

Jackson's wife, Virginia, stood just where Lebona had stood a few minutes before.

"He's not yet here, Master?"

"No." Impulsively he showed her to a chair in the kitchen. "Where else could he have gone?"

"Don't know, Master." Then she started to cry, softly. "Sunday we were together, Master, at my master's place. We talked about our children and you know one is seven and the other four and few months and firstborn is just like his father with eyes and nose and they have always been told about the zoo by playmates so they wanted to go there, so Jackson promised them he would take them to see the animals." She paused, sobbing quietly, as if she meant that to be the only way she could punctuate her speech.

"And the smaller child loves his father so and he's Jackson's favourite. You know Nkati the elder one was saying to his father the other day the day their grandmother brought them to see us — he says I wish you die, just because his father wouldn't give him more sweets. Lord he's going to be the rebel of the family and he needs a strong man's hand to keep him straight. And now if Jackson is — is — oh Lord God above."

She sobbed freely now.

"All right. I'll try my best to find him, wherever he may be. You may go now, because it's time for me to lock up."

"Thank you, Master." She left.

Stoffel stepped into the street and got into his car to drive five miles to the nearest police station. For the first time in his life he left his flat to look for a black man because he meant much to him — at any rate as a servant.

Virginia's pathetic look; her roundabout unpunctuated manner of saying things; the artless and devoted Virginia; the railway worker and his I-don't-care-whether-you're-listening manner; the picture of two children who might very well be fatherless as he was driving through the suburb; the picture of a dead man rolling down station steps and of Lebona pouring out his heart over a man he didn't know . . . These images turned round and round into a complex knot. He had got into the habit of thinking in terms of irreconcilable contradictions, oppositions and categories. Black was black, white was white — that was all that mattered.

So he couldn't at the moment answer the questions that kept bobbing up from somewhere in his soul; sharp little questions coming without ceremony; sharp little questions shooting up, sometimes like meteors, sometimes like darts, sometimes climbing up like a slow winter's sun. He was determined to resist them. He found it so much easier to think out categories and to place people.

His friend at the police station promised to help him.

The letter. Why hadn't he given it to Jackson's wife? After all, she had just as much right to possess it as her husband.

Later he couldn't resist the temptation to open the envelope; after all, it might hold a clue. He carefully broke open the flap. There were charming photographs, one of a man and woman, the other of two children, evidently theirs. They were Jackson's all right.

The letter inside was written to Jackson himself. Stoffel read it. It was from somewhere in Vendaland, from Jackson's father. He was very ill and did not expect to live much longer. Would Jackson come soon because the government people were telling him to get rid of some of his cattle to save the land from washing away, and will Jackson come soon so that he might attend to the matter because he, the old man, was powerless. He had only the strength to tell the government people that it was more land the people wanted and not less stock. He had heard the white man used certain things to stop birth in human beings, and if the white man thought he was going to do the same with his cattle and donkeys — that would be the day a donkey would give birth to a cow. But alas, he said, he had only enough strength to swear by the gods his stock wouldn't be thinned down. Jackson must come soon. He was sending the photographs which he loved very much and would like them to be safe because he might die any moment. He was sending the letter through somebody who was travelling to the gold city.

The ending was:

May the Gods bless you my son and my daughter-in-law and my lovely grandsons. I shall die in peace because I have had the heavenly joy of holding my grandsons on my knees.

It was in a very ugly scrawl without any punctuation marks. With somewhat unsteady hands Stoffel put the things back in the envelope.

Monday lunch-time Stoffel Visser motored to his flat, just to check up. He found Jackson in his room lying on his bed. His servant's face was all swollen up with clean bandages covering the whole head and cheeks. His eyes sparkled from the surrounding puffed flesh.

"Jackson!"

His servant looked at him.

"What happened?"

"The police."

"Where?"

"Victoria Police Station."

"Why?"

"They call me monkey."

"Who?"

"White man in train."

"Tell me everything, Jackson." Stoffel felt his servant was resisting him. He read bitterness in the stoop of Jackson's shoulders and in the whole profile as he sat up.

"You think I'm telling lie, Master? Black man always tell lie, eh?"

"No, Jackson. I can only help if you tell me everything." Somehow the white man managed to keep his patience.

"I take children to zoo. Coming back I am reading my night-school book. White men come into train and search everyone. One sees me reading and say what's this monkey think he's doing with a book. He tell me stand up, he shouts like its first time for him to talk to a human being. That's what baboons do when they see man. I am hot and boiling and I catch him by his collar and tie and shake him. Ever see a *marula* tree that's heavy with fruit? That's how I shake him. Other white men take me to place in front, a small room. Everyone there hits me hard. At station they push me out on platform and I fall on one knee. They lift me up and take me to police station. Not in city but far away I don't know where but I see now it must have been Victoria Station. There they charge me with drunken noise. Have you a pound? I say no and I ask them they must ring you, they say if I'm cheeky they will hell me up and then they hit and kick me again. They let me go and I walk many miles to hospital. I'm in pain." Jackson paused, bowing his head lower.

When he raised it again he said, "I lose letter from my father with my beautiful pictures."

Stoffel sensed agony in every syllable, in every gesture of the hand. He had read the same story so many times in newspapers and had never given it much thought.

He told Jackson to lie in bed, and for the first time in four years he called a doctor to examine and treat his servant. He had always sent him or taken him to hospital.

For four years he had lived with a servant and had never known more about him than that he had two children living with his mother-in-law, and a wife. Even then they were such distant abstractions — just names representing some persons, not human flesh and blood and heart and mind.

And anger came up in him to muffle the cry of shame, to

shut out the memory of recent events that was battering on the iron bars he had built up in himself as a means of protection. There were things he would rather not think about. And the heat of his anger crowded them out. What next? He didn't know. Time, time, time, that's what he needed to clear the whole muddle beneath the fog that rose thicker and thicker with the clash of currents from the past and the present. Time, time . . .

And then Stoffel Visser realized he did not want to think, to feel. He wanted to do something . . . Jackson would want a day off to go to his father . . . Sack Jackson? No. Better continue treating him as a name, not as another human being. Let Jackson continue as a machine to work for him. Meantime, he must do his duty — dispatch the commission's report. That was definite, if nothing else was. He was a white man and he must be responsible. To be white and to be responsible were one and the same thing . . .

He and the Cat

Take it to a lawyer. That's what my friend told me to do. Now, I had never had occasion to have anything to do with lawyers. Mention of lawyers always brought to my mind pictures of courts, police: terrifying pictures. Although I was in trouble, I wondered why it should be a lawyer who would help me. However, my friend gave me the address.

And from that moment my problem loomed larger. It turned in my mind. On the night before my visit to the solicitor, my heart was full of feelings of hurt. My soul fed on fire and scalding water. I'd tell the lawyer; I'd tell him everything that had gnawed inside me for several days.

I went up the stairs of the high building. Whenever I met a man I imagined that he was the lawyer and all but started to pour out my trouble. On the landing I met a boy with a man's head and face and rather large ears and lips. I told him I had come to see Mr B, the lawyer. Very gently, he told me to go into the waiting room and wait my turn with the others. I was disappointed. I had wanted to see Mr B, tell him everything, and get the lawyer's cure for it. To be told to wait . . .

They were sitting in the waiting room, the clients, ranged round the walls — about twenty of them, like those dolls ready to be bowled over at a merry-go-round fair. It didn't seem that I'd get enough time to recite the whole thing — how it all started, grew into something big, and was threatening to crush me — with so many people waiting. The boy with the man's head and face and large ears came in at intervals to call the next person. I knew what I'd do; I'd go over the whole problem in my mind, so that I could even say it backwards. The lawyer must miss nothing, nothing whatever.

But in the course of it all my eyes wandered about the room: the people, the walls, the ceiling, the furniture. A bare, unattractive room: the arms of the chairs had scratches on them that might have been made with a pin by someone who was tired of waiting. Against the only stretch of wall that was free of chairs for clients, a man of about fifty sat at a table sealing envelopes. From a picture on the wall behind him — the only picture in the room — a cat with green eyes looked down as if supervising his work. For some reason I couldn't fathom, a small school globe stood on the table. It suggested that the man sealing the envelopes might start spinning the globe to show a class that the earth is round and turns on its axis.

Once you start to make an effort to think, a thousand and one things come into your head. You would think of the previous night's adventure, perhaps; and then your girl friend might force herself into the front line; then you would begin on another trail. You might come back, as I did now, and look at the cat in front of you or the man at the table or the clients, one by one. For a fleeting moment the cat would seem to move. Then it would take up its former position, its whiskers aggressively proclaiming that you were a fool to have imagined it in motion.

You watched the frantic movements of a fly against the

window-pane, fussing to get through at the top when the bottom was open. You looked beyond to the tall buildings of the city. The afternoon heat became so oppressive that your head was just a jumble box. You didn't even hear the boy with a man's face and large ears call "Next one!" You seemed to float on the stagnant air in the room, and to be no more Sello or Temba in the flesh, waiting in a room, but a creature in the no-time of feeling and thought.

The man at the table continued with his mechanical work. He, too, seemed to want to escape from drudgery, for he spoke to two or three clients near him. And he chuckled often, showing a benignly toothless mouth. He delighted in bringing out an aphorism or proverb after every four or five sentences. "Our sages say that the only thing that you have that's surely your own is what you've already eaten, he-he-he"; "A city is beautiful from afar, but approach it and it disappoints you, he-he-he."

The clients talked in groups, discussing various things. A man was found dead near Shanty Town, killed by a train, perhaps . . . "Now, look at me; I've three sons. Do you think any one of them cares to bring home a penny? They just feed and sleep and don't care where the food comes from."

The man at the table said: "What I always say is that as soon as you allow a child to go to a dance, you've lost her."

"Try to catch a passing wind — phew!" "He cannot go far, they'll catch him." . . . "Imagine it — her husband not six months in his grave, poor man, and she takes off her mourning. That's the reward a good husband gets!"

"Our sages say a herd of cattle led by a cow always falls into the ditch . . . Listen to her always, as long as you know you have the last word . . ."

"I once met a man . . ." ". . . Potatoes? Everything is costly these days. Even a woman has gone up in price when you want to marry." . . . "Only God knows when we'll be able to go wherever we want to at any time." . . . "Are we not here because of money? Do we not walk the streets and ride on trains and buses because of money? Is money not the thing that drives us in our wanderings?"

"Death is in the leg; we walk with it, he-he-he."

"You have not been to Magaba, you say? Then you know nothing. Women selling fruit, everyone as red as the ground on which they stand; men and women just one with the red earth; salted meat roasting on the grid to be sold; red dust swirling above, people dashing this way and that like demons scorching in a fire — something like a dream."

The man at the table laughed again and said, "But horns that are put on you never stick on — so don't worry about gossip."

"We've fallen upon evil days when a girl can beat her mother-in-law." . . . "It's the first I've seen for many years. In my day a cow would give birth to a donkey if such a thing happened." . . . "Oh, everybody beats everybody these days; we're lost, lost." "But we can't go back."

"I'll know it's a zebra when I see the stripes." This from the table.

"He reads too much; the white doctors say his brain is fermenting."

"Even the eagle comes down to earth." Another proverb.

"You and I have never had the chance to go to school, so we must send our children; they'll read and write for us." . . . "Didn't you hear? They say the poor man was screaming and trying to run away before he died. He was crying and saying a mountain of sins was standing in his way." . . ."Yes, his wife stood by his bed and he said to her, he says, 'Selope, take care of my son; now give me water to drink. This is the last time,' he says, 'I shall ever ask you to do anything for me.' "

The boy with the man's face and large ears came to tell us that two white men had gone into Mr B's office. There was a moment's silence. The man at the table nodded several times. The cat glowered at him with green eyes and almost live whiskers. The fly must have found its way out. The heat was becoming a problem to reckon with.

"How many times have I come here," said an old woman to no one in particular. "In the meantime, my grand-children are starving. Their good-for-nothing father has not sent them money since the law separated him from my daughter." Deeper silence. A few people frowned at the old woman as the birds are said to have done when they were about to attack the owl. A few others seemed to be telling themselves that they weren't hearing what they were hearing.

"Where does the old mother come from?" It was some-one next to her. Once he had started he went on with a string of questions to get her off the track.

And so the people went on patching up. During all this time I had got my facts straight in my head. Several times I had imagined myself in front of Mr B: a short man with tired eyes (I always envisioned the lawyer as small in stature). I had told him everything. Now, as I sat here in the waiting room, I already knew I'd be relieved; the burden would fall off as soon as I had seen and talked to Mr B. I was so sure. It couldn't be otherwise.

There was little talking now. Fools! I thought. Their inner selves were smarting and curdling with past hurts (like mine); they were aching to see Mr B, to tell him their troubles. Yet here they were, pretending they had suspended their anxiety. Here they were, trying to rip this wave of heat and scatter it by so much gas talk: babbling away over things that didn't concern them, to cover the whirlpool of their own troubles. What was beneath these eddies and bubbles dancing and bursting on a heat wave? — someone else's possessions, flouting of the law, unfaithfulness, the forbidden tree? And the man at the table: what right had he to pronounce those aphorisms and proverbs, old as the language of man, and bleached like a brown shirt that has become a dirty white? What right had he to chuckle like that, as though he regarded us as a shopkeeper does his customers? Next one . . . the next one . . . Next!

I was left alone with the man and the cat. My heart gave a hard beat when my mind switched back to what had brought me to the lawyer. Give it to a lawyer, my friend had said confidently, as though I merely had to press an electric switch. He'll help you out of the mud. A damned good solicitor. You give him the most difficult case and he'll talk you free . . . Yes, I'd tell him everything; all that troubled my waking and sleeping hours. Then everything would be all right. I felt it would be so.

"The big man is very busy today, eh?" observed the man at the table.

"Yes," I said, mechanically.

My attention was drawn to the whole setting once more; a plain, unpretentious room with oldish chairs; the school globe; the pile of letters and envelopes; the man; and the picture of the cat.

An envelope fell to the floor. He bent down to take it up. I watched his large hands feel about for it, fumbling. Then the hand came upon the object, but with much more weight than a piece of paper warranted. Even before he came up straight in his chair I saw it clearly. The man at the table was blind, stone blind. As my eyes were getting used to the details, after my mind had thus been jolted into confused activity, I understood. Here was a man sealing envelopes, looking like a drawing on a flat surface. Perhaps he was flat and without depth, like a gramophone disc; too flat even to be hindered by the heat, the boredom of sitting for hours doing the same work; by too many or too few people coming. An invincible pair, he and the cat glowering at him, scorning our shames and hurts and the heart, seeming to hold the key to the immediate imperceptible and the remote unforseeable.

I went in to see Mr B, a small man (as I had imagined) with tired eyes but an undaunted face. I told him everything from beginning to end.

The Barber of Bariga

Bariga is a village in Lagos, Nigeria, where the author first taught, before he moved north. The dialogue is in pidgin English, an urban dialect that mixes English and vernacular words and phrases. It does not adhere to English sentence structure. People from different language groups communicate in pidgin among illiterate and semi-literate people or between these and the literate. It is a highly inventive and expressive dialect in which the speaker can take liberties with syntax and vocabulary, although one regional pidgin may vary from another throughout West Africa. There are other variations in the French-speaking countries of West Africa.

"Ha ha ha! Na be fonny worl' dees. A mahn mos' always have to lawve ay-gain un ay-gain."

Anofi turned the round head to the left with his large hand as if he were spinning a toy. The head was indeed getting out of hand as Bashiru laughed riotously. And he continued to plough through his client's hair with his clippers. Anofi came to Bashiru's house each month to "barb" his hair, as they say:

"Who be your woman dees mont', chief?" Anofi asked with tight-jawed grimness.

"Ha ha ha! A yong yong tender t'ing, my frien'."

"Bot you no be happy for your t'ree wive?"

"Yes, bot I wan' be more happy. You know what *oyingbo* say: he say de more de merry merrier merriest. Now no be vex my frien' Anofi, no be vex. I see for mirror na be so."

The barber was annoyed indeed to see the lines of his frown on the forehead. He pushed his client's head to one side with a fury-driven thumb.

"No, no be vex me. I jos' be feah."

"For wettin' you feah?"

"She be married."

"Y-yes. But no be worry she no be ole she be fresh un quick un lawvely as anyt'ing. Yes, yes, clever to make lawve and stupid for up deer." He indicated his head.

"Das for why I be feah, chief. Why no leave um de married wawn? Na be plenty woman wit'out man for dis Lagos." Anofi drew breath through his teeth to make a hissing noise as a sign of disgust.

Another shove of the head with his finger.

"Take time take time, no be vex for my head, Anofi."

"Who's she?"

"A secret."

There was a brief pause.

"People be talkin' for dis in Bariga," Anofi said.

"What people — wettin' dey talk?"

"You un som' woman."

"Dey say who?"

Anofi knew Bashiru's head very well: round with an eternal pimple on the side near the ear and an old scar in the form of a slight dent in the flesh of the skull. It was an easy head to handle for a cut. Often when Anofi propelled his clippers through the hair, he seemed to fondle the head, pushing it deftly this way and that with his thumb or forefinger. The barber seemed to own the head, as if there were a point of identity with it, as if he would be hurt if someone else gave it a haircut. As his clippers nibbled down the slopes, he seemed conscious of his physical ease and pleasure in a job well done.

The barber put the finishing touches, and Bashiru looked tidy. He grunted approval, like a purring over-sized cat that is being stroked, when Anofi held the mirror behind for him to see the trimming effects at the back of his head.

"T'ank you," Bashiru said, giving the barber three shillings and adjusting his *agbada*. "*Odabo*, sah — remain in peace."

Anofi went out into the sun. He knew his father would be entertaining the waiting customers in his shop with some of his funny stories.

For the last ten years or so Anofi's father had come to sit in the shop while the barber worked. The old man featured in his memory mostly in the posture in which he sat on the bench in the shop: one leg bent and resting almost entirely on the bench; the other bent leg shooting up vertically so that he could plant his elbow on the knee and prop up the head with his open palm. The old man often struck that pose when he was sure what he said would be regarded as expert counsel or a statement that could brook no argument. He was more often sure than not, and he seldom failed to raise an argument with the clients. Each morning he came into the shop through the back door, shuffled his feet to the front door, looking cool in his *buba*, and surveyed the street life. Then he turned round and went to take his post on the bench.

Often Anofi's old man spoke in a monotone, apparently not caring whether anyone was listening or not. Or he chewed away at his kola nut, his jaws moving like a goat's. Indeed there was something goatlike about his face, altogether; he also sneezed as weakly and coughed as fussily as a goat. When he smiled to deride an argument, he would emphasize this by stretching out his lips so as to push out bits of kola nut with the inside lining of his cheeks so they should not escape the onslaught of his scattered molars. In the process, his rusty-coloured front teeth came into full view, looking like the remaining few pillars of a demolished building.

Anofi went on with his work, seldom turning round to engage in conversation with his father. When he was

working, his father hovered somewhere in his subconscious or somewhere on the fringe of awareness. On
one of the few occasions when father and son exchanged
ideas, the older man said in the middle of the morning, "I'm
sure if you collected all the hair you cut off and found
someone to buy it, you would get rich." He chewed his
stick for cleaning his teeth.

"Rich — how, Papa?"

"I don't know why the white man cannot use people's
hair."

"Why, Papa?"

"The white people use sheep's hair, the hair of wild
animals."

Now he moved his stick, which had split into broom-like
bristles at the end, in vertical strokes. All this gave his
words a sarcastic ring he might not have intended them to
contain.

"Are you joking, Papa?"

"No."

"But people's hair is so dirty." Anofi's body twitched
from a sensation of disgust.

"The white man can do many things. He can make
machines to wash the hair. The white man seems to be
clever."

"Why always white man, white man? Cannot the black
man do these things?" Anofi said in spite of his disgust.

"What machines have we ever made?"

"But we use them very well. You, Papa, you are like the
woman who came out of the office of the dentist and said to
us who were waiting, '*Oyingbo* — the white man is
wonderful, he has made things to take out a tooth without
pain.' And you know who had taken out her tooth? A black

woman doctor. Oho, you are like that."

There was a moment of silence while the client was shaking off hair from his clothes, slapping the back of his neck several times. Then he straightened up. Looking at Anofi's father he took out a ballpoint pen. "Look," the customer said. He pressed the end of the protruding stick in so that the writing tip shot out. He pressed the clip and the tip disappeared. He repeated the operation a few times and then said: "Na whitemahn na wonderful-o. Look wettin' he make!" He smiled and walked out, leaving Anofi in fits of laughter from which he only recovered several minutes later. Papa looked upset and, to express it, he noisily sucked air through the central gap between the top biting teeth in order to push in a morsel of kola nut.

Most times Anofi said very little, and looked exasperatingly unruffled. It seemed that he never wanted to stir up things. He seemed incapable of nervous tension, of anger or malice.

He saw much of what happened in the street through the window. Masqueraders passed by, frightening children and beating drums, sprawling all over the place and prancing as if they itched to do something desperate or exciting. "They are looking for fun, and they will get it," Anofi would say to himself. Wedding and funeral processions passed by, and groups of women in party uniform — on all these, he seldom voiced a comment. He consciously or unconsciously refused to be emotionally involved, seeming to despise the whole show. He did not, however, despise it. He liked much of the music booming out of the loudspeaker in the opposite shop where they played gramophone records or had the radio on throughout the day.

The current high-life favourite was "Corner Love". The vocalist said how much he disliked "corner love" and mistrusted it. He warned the young women against the lad who drew her onto a street corner to propose love. "I no like corner-corner love," the singer insisted forebodingly. One customer thought the singer was wasting his time and vocal energy, because "na be no corner-lawve for dis Lagos, a-ah! He jos tok-tok for not'ing cawm out ot for his head. If to say you hask 'im he woul'n't know."

One Saturday morning a car drove down the street with a white couple in it. Anofi was moving towards his signboard EXPERT BARBAR to adjust it (the "r" in *expert* perched on top of the "e" and "t" with a sign to indicate that the signwriter had forgotten it, or simply had not known it should be there). He saw the car stop at the crossroads and a cyclist drive into a wedge between the car and a wall. Just then, the car moved again. To Anofi, who had stopped short in front of his signboard, it was quite clear that the cyclist was going to be in trouble. The bumper caught the spokes of the front wheel. The rider, unseated, was suspended in air for a split second, his *agbada* ballooning as he made the forced landing, with a cry, "What ees wrong!" The driver pulled up short in the middle of the cross-street on sensing the trouble, by which time Anofi had a seizure of torrential laughter, such as he was never known to have the capacity for. He did not move away from the signboard, but clung to one of the two poles holding it up, as if he were afraid he would take off.

In a short time a number of people had gathered at the place of the accident. The white man was having an argument with the cyclist who was claiming money for repairs. Always people gathered around a place where something was happening that was not daily routine: a man changing a tyre; a petrol attendant checking tyres; a motorist stopping to drink tea out of a flask, and so on. Whenever there had been an accident, the crowd had many observations and opinions to air, far more of the latter than the former.

The white man soon felt overwhelmed by the presence of the chattering and murmuring crowd and anger was beginning to choke him. The cyclist was now clearly crying. Small children pointed fingers at him and giggled. He looked at his *agbada* in between complaining and claiming compensation.

Suddenly the white woman came out of the car. She seemed beside herself with fury. She started to drag her husband back to the car, shouting to the cyclist the while: "Go to the police then, go to the police and have us arrested, but you're getting not a farthing out of us!" She paused as the husband was not coming readily. Then again, "Why don't you go and report the matter if you're not satisfied? You came in between the car and the fence." Dropping her voice a little, "Let's go, Andrew, let's go. Come, come into the car. We've got to go, we haven't got time to waste listening to this silly talk."

The man Andrew put the brakes on somewhere in his legs. He was tall and thin, and his small head was swaying above all the others. His face was a deep pink from unchecked perspiration. He was also suppressing an itching sensation in one of his now wet armpits. He felt if he scratched it now it would blunt the edge of the point he was trying to make, like suddenly coughing in the middle or at the beginning of a venomous phrase during a quarrel or a reprimand. Perhaps he did not want to feel that he had arbitrarily decided that he was in the right if in fact the other man was. And then there was a chance that they might both be wrong or right. Moreover, the other man's crying act was embarrassing him.

"No go say I um seely," the cyclist barked.

"I think you're just being silly," the woman insisted.

"Joo can't abuse me like dat, a-ah! It's un insolt. I say joo can't abuse me. Um not your stewart."

"No, you're too silly to be anybody's stewart."

"A-ah, she's abusing me ay-gain, a-ah! Do you hear-hear-ah?" Then he broke into Yoruba, definitely appealing to the sensibilities of the crowd.

"Slap her!" someone shouted.

"If not to say she's a woo-man I coul' 'ave slapped her. But what is she besides — just *oyingbo.*"

The woman, realizing that Andrew was not obeying her command, left the crowd and walked towards Anofi, who was still standing by the signboard. He had only just recovered from his fit of laughing.

"You were looking at us as we were coming on, what did you see? Please tell them what you saw." *Them* referred to the crowd, just as if she had begun to accept the incident as a communal concern.

They looked in the direction of the barber-shop.

Anofi shrugged his narrow shoulders, shook his head, "I never know, I never see not'ing, I mean moch." And he walked into his shop.

The woman gave a deep sigh and she said to Andrew again, "Let's go, it'll do us no good talking like this."

"Let's give the man ten shillings for his repairs."

"Over my dead body!"

He took out the money and walked towards the cyclist

with his arm outstretched.

"Andrew, come here! Don't just give away money like that!"

He was just barely able to hear the cyclist say: "T'ank you. Na we be frien's now." There was loud cheering from the group of people as though an armistice had been declared. He went to join his protesting wife in the car, feeling anything but heroic.

"Between that wretched lying barber and your stupid self," she said, "the devil alone knows how these people mean to build a nation."

"That's a problem for the nation-builders, darling. Besides, how can you be sure that simply because a man was looking at us, as you say the barber was doing, he must have seen what happened?"

"Oh, he knows he did." She looked in the direction of the shop door, and saw that Anofi was looking at them. "The African always wins when those of his kind are in authority."

"It's *our* turn to learn the lesson, darling."

And the car shot forward.

There must have been several times when Anofi himself could not say whether he had actually seen what he thought he had seen, or when in his perpetual mood of detachment he told himself that he was not seeing what he was seeing. When a blind beggar came to his door, he dug his hand into his pocket, took out a coin and, as if in a dream, walked to the door and dropped it in the beggar's enamel bowl. Three blind women might stop at his door with children on their backs. They would wail their incantations to Allah with heartrending effect, so that Anofi's father's jaws pounded harder on the kola nut and, with the aid of his tongue, drew air through the side teeth to hiss his bewilderment and pride. Anofi, for his part, usually went to the door in a kind of tremor to tell the party to move away. On approaching them, he saw their grey, lifeless and solicitous eyes quivering beneath the eyelids, and he saw their red teeth and the footprints of small-pox on their faces. And something deep-deep down in the pit of his stomach would stir. He would give something and return quickly to his customer.

"These beggars!" a customer would sometimes say. "Dey give too moch troble, a-ah! Dey be blind un dey go born piccin, a-ah! Foolish nort'erner woman." Anofi would keep mute, some chord inside him still quivering.

About a month after the last haircut Anofi gave Bashiru, the man of property, a large man entered the shop and literally threw himself onto a bench near Anofi's father. He was quite out of breath. Anofi's old father felt very tiny near such a mountain of man, and it irritated him.

"Have you ever hear soch a t'ing, Anofi," Okeke puffed out. "I go kill him, true, believe me I go slaughter dat man. He goes ay-bout wit' a dead title, dead-dead title and rascally t'ings."

"Who's dat?" Anofi asked.

"Bashiru."

"Wettin' he don'?"

"He t'ink becos na he be rich," and he began ticking the items off on his sausage-like fingers, "he got plenty moni, plenty houses, plenty upstairs, plenty wives, plenty piccin, plenty farm, so he can't keep his man inside for pants for his wives only. Even he take oder people's wives too."

"Bot wettin he don?"

"Look um. His gran-dad don' eat his chief's title. His dad don' try to force it out to be made chief un he don' fail. Bot his dad was clever un he don' take oder people's houses un moni. He don' t'ief t'ief everyt'ing un now his son Bashiru take de blod of t'ief from his dad un t'ief t'ief wife un moni un houses all over now he be fat un rich . . ."

"Wettin he don'?"

"Foolish mahn, I tell him what Bashiru don' don' un he still hask what he don', a-ah! Na you be no idi-awt, Anofi." He rose to take the chair for a cut. "Bashiru be tryin' to t'ief my wife."

"Your wife na she be wantin' to be t'iefed?"

"You make me vex, Anofi. How can my wife want to be t'iefed? Don't tell me you don't know ay-bout it. Everybody in Bariga knows it."

The answer startled Anofi. He had heard Bashiru boast about his latest exploit, but he would never have thought that Okeke's wife would be so foolish as to be seduced.

"Moni ay-gain, you see for dat? Now I know Bashiru has been takin' my wife when I'm wo'kin' in town. Believe me I go kill dat mahn. I no sleep at night becos of wawry, I don't chop becos of wawry and Bashiru chop chop bellyful becos he no wawry."

"Please no be too vex I beg you Okeke. No be good to kill-o. Jos' beat him das all."

Okeke's neck stiffened, and Anofi had to wait a few seconds before he could turn the man's head to a desired angle. So he did it, that Bashiru, he thought. Okeke's voice filled him with unhappy thoughts.

For a reason he could not explain he felt he was being sucked into the affair between the three persons. He did not know what was happening to him, and he did not seem to have the power to resist being sucked in. When Okeke left, he and his father looked at each other for a spell, as if their thoughts had found a confluence and were rushing down the same mainstream, and there was nothing more to say about it.

When two days later a message came to Anofi that Bashiru had died by accident at a wedding, he sensed evil in the air. He was called to come and shave Bashiru's head to prepare him for burial, according to the rules of a religious cult to which the deceased belonged. He soon found himself in the death room. The group of people in there made way for him to pass and kneel beside the corpse. He sat down and put the head on his lap. The thought that this head, the contour lines of which he knew so well, was now like a stone, made him shiver. When there was still a patch of hair left, Anofi's clippers struck against something hard. He ran his clippers against the obstacle once more and the sound told him it was metal. He shaved around it until it emerged: the head of a nail that told him in no doubtful terms that it was a long thick one.

With a sudden movement the barber lifted up the head onto the pillow on the floor, jumped up and said to the people in the room: "Why you no go tell me dat dis man was killed de way of a t'ief?" He did not wait for a reply but dashed out of the house. Outside he stood still in the street. He stood like a man who, feeling a fever coming on, seems to be tuning in to the mechanism that is the body in an attempt to feel the throb of it, perhaps to reassure himself. Then he walked on.

Dusk was creeping in, but from the elevated end of the street where Anofi was, the rusted iron roofs of Bariga's houses were still clearly defined in all their recklessly uneven outlines. Shopkeepers and petty street traders were pumping their pressure lamps. Soon lights would be exploding in various places from candles, pressure lamps and other manual contraptions. People coming in from Lagos where they worked. Anofi only faintly heard the continuous roar of human noises, absorbed as he was in other things.

"Make we walk togeder," someone said coming from a side-street.

Anofi merely looked at Okeke and walked on.

"You cawmin' from Bashiru's house?"

"Yes." He was not sure whether he wanted to talk to someone or not. "You don' kill man, Okeke."

"Som' people dey don' kill um."

"You don' kill man, Okeke," Anofi repeated, as if his mind pounded at regular intervals, heedless of any other sound.

"Som' people not me. But he don' die way na he want."

"You don' kill a *mahn!* A *mahn*, you don't take de life of a man to buy de lawve of a woman. Na be what kind of lawve dis? Not to say you can't beat your woman for stick, you savvy? You can beat woman un kick her if she sleep for anoder man's bed, beat her un send her to hospitule. Na she got madness for head un hotness for flesh you can kick dem ot, dis madness and hotness. Not to kill anoder man a-ah." He looked straight ahead of him all the time, as if there were no one beside him.

His insistence irritated Okeke, and even made him uncomfortable. But he wasn't going to be frightened out of his course. All the time they walked on without looking at each other.

"Das how dey kill t'iefman for my contry," Okeke said gloatingly but with self-confidence. "Bashiru don' t'ief som't'ing for somebody."

"Un you don' send um to kill."

"Jos savvy me, Anofi, I no wan' no palaver me son of Okeke. I hate big mahn strong mahn who eats from hand of de poor people, take wife for people wi'out no moni, fat mahn who chop chop bellyful moni dat is oder people's own. Now he t'inks he's God almighty un he wan' chop oder people's wives, a-ah!"

"Na you hate him becos he was rich and fat not becos he don' t'ief your woman?"

"Is for same t'ing Anofi. You no be borned yesternight. Is same t'ing. Poor man t'ief small small becos he's afraid for big moni, rich man t'ief big becos he got protec-shon un he buy policemahn."

"Un your wife be fool woman un cheap if she stand for de middle of de road for him to jomp on top of her."

"If not to say you be my frien' I coul' 'ave feel vex. Bot even you know Bashiru is not jos any cock. He got moni and no woman fit for say no when she moni in front of her eyes."

"How you t'ink you escape police?"

"Moni for his pocket un he shot op for mout' and let his tongue sleep."

"Even you don' get rich now, you? Okeke, dis is a big terrible t'ing. Even I nevah know what I go say for police an dey hask me . . ."

"Only what you saw for inside, his big dead head. Make you say not'ing pass dat at-all-at-all-at-all."

"Why?"

"Becos Bashiru he don't make lawve for your wife too, idi-awt! Wake op! She waitin' to tell you for house. See you nex' tomorrow."

Okeke left him.

Many things began to make sense to him. He saw his wife's beauty for what it was. Indeed she leapt into his awareness as she had seldom ever done in her physical form. This rediscovery of her loveliness fused with the anger in him so that the world around him seemed so small, so overcrowded.

He made a detour without meaning to, often running into dead ends. He felt numb. "Tomorrow," he said aloud in his language and with an air of finality, "we must go away from this place. The whole house."

And as Anofi walked on, radio music exploded from a nearby shop and set his nerves quivering:

No moni, no bus,
Even na you be clever
     pass every-wawn:
No moni, no bus.

A Ballad of Oyo

Oyo is an old city in Nigeria. It has some of the most famous markets in the country.

Ishola (also called Mama-Jimi because her first son was Jimi) found a tramp on her counter slab at Oyo's central market, where she took her stand each day to sell vegetables and fruit. Furiously she poked the grimy bundle with a broom to tell him a few things he had better hear: *there are several other places where he could sleep; she sells food off this counter, not fire-wood — like him; so he thought to lie on a cool slab on a hot night, eh? — Why does he not sleep under a running tap?* And so on. With a sense of revulsion she washed the counter.

These days, when market day began, it also meant that Ishola was going to have to listen to her elder sister's endless prattling during which she spun words and words about the younger sister being a fool to keep a useless husband like Balogun in food and clothing. Off and on, for three months, Ishola had tried to fight against the decision to tell Balogun to go look for another wife while she went her own way. Oh, why did her sister have to blabber like this? Did her sister think that she, Ishola, liked being kicked about by her man? Her sister might well go on like this, but she could not divine the burning questions that churned inside Ishola.

That is right, Ishola, her sister who sold rice next to her, would say. *You are everybody's fool, are you not? Lie still like that and let him come and sit and play drums on you and go off and get drunk on palm wine, come back and beat you, scatter the children — children of his palm-wine-stained blood* (spitting), *like a hawk landing among chicks, then you have no one to blame only your stupid head* (pushing her other breast forcibly into her baby's mouth for emphasis). *How long has he been giving you so much pain like this? How long are you going to try to clean a pig that goes back into the mud? You are going to eat grass very soon, you will tell me — and do not keep complaining to me about his ways if my advice means nothing to you.*

And so goes the story of Ishola, Ishola who was called Mama-Jimi, a mother of three children. Slender, dark-and-smooth-skinned, with piercing eyes that must have seen through dark nights.

Day and night the women of Oyo walk the black road, the road of tarmac, to and from the market. They can be seen walking, riding the dawn, walking into sunrise; figures can be seen, slender as twilight; their feet feel every inch of the tarmac, but their wares press down on the head and the neck takes the strain, while the hips and legs propel the body forward. A woman here, a woman there in the drove has her arm raised in a loop, a loop of endurance, to support the load, while the other arm holds a suckling child in a loop, a loop of love. They must walk fast, almost at a trot, so that they may not feel the pain of the weight so much.

The week before Mama-Jimi had started for Oyo Market, her body feeling the seed of another child grow that had not yet begun to give her sweet torment, bitter ecstasy in the stomach. The night before he left, her husband had told her he was going to the north to see his other wives. He would come back — when? *When he was full of them and they of him,* Mama-Jimi knew. *When he should have made sure that the small trade each was doing went well,* he said.

Mama-Jimi looked at his shadow quivering on the wall in the light of the oil lamp as he stooped over her, and loneliness swept over her in a flood. They loved and they remained a promontory rising above the flood. And Mama-Jimi again took her place in the order of things: one of three wives giving all of her to one she loved and taking what was given by her man with a glad heart. Oyo will always be Oyo; whatever happens to it, the market will always be there, come rain, come blood, come malaria.

It was the week before, only the week before, when the rain caught the market women on the tarmac to market. The sky burst and the rain came down with power. It rumbled down the road in rivulets. Mama-Jimi felt the load inside become heavy, knotting up beneath her navel. Her feet became heavy, the hips failed to twist. But she tried to push on. She could see the others way ahead through the grey of the rain. Mama-Jimi's thoughts were on the market, the market of Oyo: she must reach it. For if she should fall, she thought, or feel sicker, other women were there.

But the woman sagged and fell and dragged herself out of the road. She felt the blood oozing, warm and cold. A life was running out of her, she was sure of it.

A life dead just as soon as born and sprouting . . .

Two women found her on the roadside, cold, wet.

Whispers bounced and rebounded at the market that Mama-Jimi was dead, dead, Mama-Jimi was gone, gone in the rain. But it was not as whispers told it.

Did she know it was there?

Ehe, she did, she told me so.

And her man gone to the north, a-ah? So it is said.

Are they going to call him? They must. Only yesterday night we were together and she was glad she was going to give her man a third child.

To die when your people are far, far away from you, a-ah!

We are most of us strangers here.

It is true.

This was a week before, and the market at Oyo jingles and buzzes and groans, but it goes on as it has done for many years since the first Alafin came here.

You know what the market is like every morning, not so? Babbling tongues, angry tongues, silent tongues. Down there a woman was suckling a baby while she sold. Near to Ishola a woman was eating *gari* and *okaran* and gravy out of a coloured enamel bowl. Someone else next to her handled her sales for her. As the heat mounted a lad was pouring water on bunches of lettuce to keep them from wilting and thus refusing to be sold. But the lad seemed to be wilting himself, because as soon as he leaned back against a pole, sleep seized him and his head tilted back helplessly like a man having a shave in a barber's chair.

The mouth opened and the lettuce lost its importance for a while. Mostly *oyingbo* — white people — came to buy lettuce. On and off while he slept, someone sprinkled water over his face, stared at the lettuce and then poured water on it. Some fat women opposite Ishola's counter were shouting and one seldom knew whether they were angry or simply zealous. They also splashed water over the pork they were selling so as to keep away blue flies that insisted on sitting on it. All the would-be buyers who stood at the pork counter fingered the pieces; they lifted them up, turned them round, put them back, picked them up again. There was no exchange of smiles here.

Ten shillings, said the pork woman who herself seemed to have been wallowing in grease.

Four shillings, suggested the customer.

Eight shillings last.

Five (taking it and putting it back as if disgusted).

Seven las' price.

With a long-drawn sound between the teeth to signify disgust, the customer left. The pork woman looked at her fellow-vendor, as if to say, stupid customers!

Oyingbo women did not buy meat at these markets.

They said they were appalled by the number of hands that clutched it. They bought imported meat in the provision stores at prices fixed seemingly to annoy expatriates. One missionary woman had been known to bring a scale for the vendor to weigh the meat in order to get her money's worth. What, she had exclaimed, you don't weigh meat in this market? Ridiculous! The meat women had looked baffled. The next time the missionary brought her own balance. This time *they* thought something was ridiculous, and they laughed to show it. Even after weighing a piece, she found that she still had to haggle and bargain. Enthusiasm had flagged on her part, and after this, she only came to the market to rescue some of the lettuce and parsley from continual drenching and to buy fruit.

So did the other white women. One of them turned round in answer to a shout from a vendor. Custumah, custumah! She approached Ishola's counter where there were heaps of carrots and tomatoes. She was smiling, as one is expected to do from behind a counter.

Nice car-*rot* madam.

How much?

Shilling (picking up a bunch).

Sixpence.

No madam, shilling (smiling).

Sixpence.

Ha-much madam wan' pay? (with no smile).

All right, seven pence.

Ni'pence.

Seven.

No 'gree, madam (smiling).

The customer realized that she had come to the end of the road. She yielded, but not before saying, ninepence is too much for these.

A-ah madam. If not to say madam she buy for me many times I coul' 'ave took more moni for you.

Towards sunset Ishola packed up. She had made up her mind to go to Bab Dejo, the president of the court of the local authority. She firmly believed that the old man had taken a bribe. Either her father-in-law or Balogon himself, her delinquent husband, could have offered it. This, she believed, must be the reason why the court would not hold a hearing of her case against her husband. Twice Ishola had asked him to hear her case. Each time the old man said something to delay it. The old fox, she thought. This time, she fixed simply on putting five pounds in front of the president. He cannot refuse so much money, Ishola thought. But go back to that animal of a husband, never — *no more, he is going to kill me one of these days I do not want to die I do not want to die for nothing I want to work for my children I want to send them to school I do not want them to grow old on the market place and die counting money and finding none. Baba Dejo just take the money he must listen to my case and let the law tell Balogun to leave me alone with the children and go his way I will go mine I know his father has gone and bribed him to keep the matter out of the court and why? Because he does not want to lose his son's children and because − I do not know, he is very fond of me he has always stood up for me against his son − yes he loves me but I am married to his son not to him and his love does not cure his son's self-made madness. Lijadu loves me and I want him let my heart burst into many pieces if he does not take me as his wife I want him because he has such a pure heart.*

Ishola was thinking of the day Lijadu came to fetch her in his car and they went to Ijebude for that weekend of love and heartbreaks: heartbreaks because she was someone else's wife, someone who did not care for her and even then had gone to Warri without telling her. Now Lijadu was ready to give Balogun the equivalent of the bride price he had paid to Ishola's parents and so release her to become his wife. Balogun and his father had refused Lijadu's money.

Just what irritates me so, Ishola thought. I could burst into a hundred parts so much it fills me with anger. So they want to stop me from leaving their useless son, useless like dry leaves falling from a tree. Just this makes me mad and I feel I want to stand in the middle of the road and shout so as everyone can hear me. That man! − live with him again? He beats me he leaves me no money he grows fat on my money he does not care for the children the children of his own own blood from his very own hanging things . . .

I wonder how much the old man will want? The thought flashed across Ishola's mind, like a streak of lightning that rips across the milling clouds, illuminating the sky's commotion all the more.

If your father-in-law Mushin were not my friend, says the president of the court, Dejo, when Ishola tells him the business of her visit, I should not let you come and speak to me on a matter like this. It is to be spoken in court only.

You do not want me to bring it to court sir.

I would do it if —

How much, sir?

Give me what you have, my daughter. He looks disdainful in the face as he says so. It does not please the young woman. He takes five pounds in paper money from her hand.

What is this I hear from your father-in-law, that you want to leave your husband? Ishola feels resentful at the thought that her case must have been chewed dead by these old men. But she presses the lid hard to keep her feelings from bubbling over. I beg that you listen, sir, she says. Balogun beats me he does not work he eats and sleeps he does not care for the children of his own-own blood, sir, he drinks too much palm wine this is too much I have had a long heart to carry him so far but this is the end of everything no no this is all I can carry.

Is he a man in bed?

Not when he is drunk and that is many times sir. She was looking at the floor at this time.

Hm, that is bad that is bad my child, that is bad. What does he say when you talk to him about his ways?

Nothing, sir. He just listens he listens and just listens that is all.

A man has strange ways and strange thoughts.

There is silence.

So he drinks himself stupid. I know there are certain places in Oyo where you can hear the name of Balogun spoken as if he were something that smells very bad. So he drinks himself stupid until he is too flabby to do his work in bed, a-ah! How many children have you by the way?

Three, sir.

The youngest is how old?

Two years, sir.

If a man gets too drunk to hoe a field another man will and he shall regret, he will see. He seems to be talking to himself. But a man who comes home only as a he-goat on heat, the old man continues, and not as a helper and father is useless. I will tell him that I will tell Balogun that myself. Animals look for food for their mates and their brood, why cannot a man?

You have talked to him twice before, sir.

Oh yes oh yes I have my child I know.

Silence.

But your father-in-law Mushin loves you so much so much my child.

I love him too but I am his son's wife not his.

You speak the truth there.

Silence.

It would break his heart all the same. Look at it whichever way you like. You fill a space left in his heart by the death of his wife and often defiled by the deeds of a worthless son. Dejo's face is one deep shadow of gravity.

I do not like that boy Balogun not one little moment, he goes on, but his father will weep because he holds you like his own-own daughter.

Ishola's head is full of noises and echoes of noises, for she has heard all this a few times before. She has determined her course and she shall not allow her tender sentiments to take her out of it, she mustn't, no not now. Perhaps after, when tender feelings will be pointless. She still bears a little love for Balogun, but she wants her heart to be like a boulder so as not to give way.

Let me go and call my wife to talk with you more about this, old Dejo says as he leaves the room. As he does so, he stretches out his hand to place a few crumpled notes of money in Ishola's hand, whispering your heart is kind, my child, it is enough that you showed the heart to give, so take it back.

Ishola feels a warm and cold air sweep over and through her. She trembles a little and she feels as if something were dangling in space and must fall soon.

Old Dejo's wife enters, round-bellied: the very presence of life's huge expectation.

But — such an old man, Ishola thinks . . .

I can see it in her eyes Balogun I can see it in her eyes, Mushin said in his son's house one morning. Ishola is going to leave us.

She is at the market now, Papa. She loves me too much to do a foolish thing like that.

When are you going to wake up you useless boy, he gasped, as he had often done before. What kind of creature was given me for a son! What does your mother say from the other world to see you like this!

Balogun poured himself palm wine and drank and drank and drank. I can see the blade of a cutlass coming to slash at my heart, the older man said. I can feel it coming.

Go and rest father, you are tired.

And Balogun walked out into the blazing shimmering sun, stopped to buy cigarettes at a small stall on the roadside and walked on, the very picture of aimlessness.

When are you going to stop fooling like this with Balogun I ask you, Ishola's sister said rasping out as she sat behind her counter. Her baby who was sucking looked up into her face with slight but mute concern in its eyes.

She does not know she does know this woman she . . . will never know she will know what I am made of . . .

I would never allow a man to come stinking of drink near me in the blankets (spitting). I told you long ago to go to court and each time you allow that old Dejo with his fat wife to talk you out of it. Are you a daughter of my father?

Oh what a tiresome tongue sister has . . . You wait, you just wait . . .

Just a black drunken swine that is what he is. A swine is even better because it can look for rubbish to eat. Balogun does not know what people are he would not go a long way with me no he would not he does not know people. Eat sleep and lay a pile of dung, eat sleep and lay a pile of dung while men of his age group are working: the woman who gave birth to that man . . .

Sister! Leave that poor woman to lie quiet in her grave.

I will but not that wine-bloated creature called Balogun.

Lijadu must not forget to send Mushin's money of the bride-price . . .

That piece of pork? a customer asked.

Ten shillings.

Five.

Nine.

Six.

No 'gree.

Six and six.

No 'gree.

Six and six.

No 'gree. Eight, las' price.

Seven.

No 'gree.

And the market roar and chatter and laughter and exclamations and smells put together seemed to be a live symphony quite independent of the people milling around.

Black shit! Ishola's sister carried on . . .

Ishola was out of Oyo in the evening, going towards Oshogbo with her three children. Lijadu would follow the next day and join them in a small village thirty miles out so as to make pursuit fruitless. Lijadu joined her at noon the next day, looking pale and blue and shaken.

What is it with you Lijadu? Why are you so pale? Are you sick?

Silence.

Lijadu what is it?

He sat on the ground and said Mushin has passed away. He passed away about midnight. One of the neighbours found him lying cold in the passage. People say they heard him cry the last time: Ishola, my grandchildren!

Ishola could not move for a few moments. She seemed frozen cold cold cold.

At break of day each morning you will see the women of Oyo with their baskets on their heads. You can see them on the black tarmac going to the market, their bodies twisting at the hip the strong hip. You can see their feet feel their way on the dark tarmac as they ride the dawn, riding into daylight. The figures are slender as twilight. You can see Ishola, too, because she came back, came back to us. She told us that when she heard of the death of her father-in-law she thought, this is not good for my future life with Lijadu I will go back to that cripple . . .

A Point of Identity

It was not until a crisis broke upon Karel Almeida that I began to wonder how he had come to live with us in Corner B location, seven miles out of Pretoria. It was first rumoured that he must be well-to-do. Then people said he *was* rich. And then people went around saying that he had won a huge bet at the race course wherever (no-one cared to know where exactly) it was he had come from. Soon it was said that he was a coloured African. And then again they said, *ag*, he's not "coloured", just one of these blacks with funny names. All these guesses arose from the fact that Karel Almeida was light in complexion, large in physique, and had improved the appearance of his three-roomed house within two months or so of his arrival. Also, Almeida laughed a lot, like "a man who had little to worry him". But I shouldn't forget to add that he was a bachelor when he arrived, and must have been saving up and living light.

This was little less than ten years ago — I mean when he came to our street and occupied a house next door to mine.

During those years Karel Almeida became "Karel" to me and my wife and "Uncle Karel" or "Uncle Kale" to the children. We were very fond of each other, Karel and I. We had got to take each other for granted, so it was normal for him, when he was spending his two weeks' leave at home and my wife fell ill, to look after her and cook for her and give her medicines while I was away at school, teaching. He worked in a Jew's motor-mechanic shop in the city, and lived austerely enough.

Karel's whole physical being seemed to be made of laughter. When he was going to laugh, he shook and quivered as if to "warm up" for a take-off and then the laugh was released like a volley from deep down his large tummy, virtually bullying the listener to join in the "feast".

"Hm, just hear how Karel is eating laughter!" my wife would say when the sound issued from Karel's house.

"Me my mudder was African, my farder was Portugalese," Karel often said in conversation. "Not, mind you, de Portugalese what come an' fuck aroun' an' have a damn good time an' den dey vamoose off to Lourenco Marques. But de ole man went to LM an' he got sick." After a pause he burst out, "An' he die sudden, man, just like you blow a candle out, T." He always called me "T" which was an intimate way of referring to me as a schoolteacher.

"Where were you and your mother?"

"In Jo'burg, man. It's now — let me see — one, two, three, *ja,* three years. Died in Sibasa, man, way up nort' Transvaal. My Ma nearly died same day and followed my Pa de day he die. Fainted an' gave us hell to bring her back. She went to LM for de funeral."

"And now, where's she?"

"Who, my mudder? She's dead — let me see — one, two, two years now. I brought her wit' me to Jo'burg when I was learning mechanics at de same garage what brought me here. Good Jew boss, very good. He got a son at university in Jo'burg. Nice boy too. My Ma didn't like Jo'burg not dis much, so I took her back to Sibasa."

We often teased each other, Karel and I, he was so full of laughter.

"I can't understand," I said one day, "why you cycle to work and back instead of taking a bus. Just look how the rain beats on you and the wind almost freezes you in winter." He laughed.

"Trouble wit' you kaffirs is you's spoiled."

"And you Boesmans and Hotnotte are tough, you'll tell me."

"An' de Coolies, too. See how dey walk from house to house selling small t'ings. Dey's like donkeys, man. Can't catch dem coolies, man. You and me will never catch dem. It's *dey* who'll always make de money while we Hotnotte an' kaffirs sleep or loaf about or stick a knife or plug a bullet into someone or jes' work for what we eat an' live in an' laugh at life. Jeeslike man, dey's gone dose Coolies, dey'll beat us at makin' money all de time."

"But Hotnotte, Boesmans and Kaffirs and Coolies are all frying in the same pan, boy, and we're going to sink or swim together, you watch."

"OK. Kaffir, let's swim."

"What you got, Boesman?"

"Whisky, gin and lime. But you know, I'm not a Hottentot or a Bushman, I've got European blood straight from de balls no zigzag business about it." And, as he served the drinks, his laughter rang pure and clear and solid.

"But serious now, true's God, I've always lived wit' Africans an' never felt watchimball, er, discomfortable or ashamed." He could never say "what you call it". "Damn it all man, if my farder slept wit' mudder an' dey made me dat's dey business. You, T, your great-great-greatgrandmudder may have been white or brown woman herself. How can you be sure of anyt'ing? How can any Indian be sure he's hundred percent India? I respec' a man what respec' me no matter his colour."

He spoke with vehemence and compassion.

Karel took an African woman to live with him as his wife. She was a lovely woman whose background was unknown. She was hardworking and Karel treated her with great affection. She never had much to say, but she was not proud, only shy.

And the crisis came.

If the whole thing did not begin to set members of a family against one another or individual persons against their communities or vice versa; if it did not drive certain people to the brink of madness and to suicide; if it did not embarrass very dark-skinned people to sit in front of a white tribunal and have to claim "mixed parentage", then we should have thought that someone had deliberately gone out of his way to have fun in creating it. The white people who governed the country had long been worried about the large numbers of coloured Africans who were fair enough to want to play white, and of Africans who were fair enough to want to try for "coloured". They had long been worried about the prospect of one coffee-coloured race which would shame what they called "white civilization" and the "purity" of their European blood. So, maybe, after a sleepless night someone ate his breakfast, read his morning newspapers in between bites, walked about his suburban garden, told his black "boy" to finish cleaning his car, kissed his wife and children goodbye ("don't expect me for supper, dear"), went to the House of Assembly and began to propel a huge legislative measure through the various formal stages to the President's desk where it would be signed as law. Whatever happened, a board was established to re-classify coloured Africans to decide whether they were to remain on the register as "coloureds" or "natives". All people who said that they were "coloured" had to go to the board for "tests".

They were ordered to produce evidence to prove their ancestry. (Was there a white man or woman in the family tree or not?) The onus was clearly on the subject of the inquiry to prove that he was "coloured". Day after day papers were filed: birth certificates; photographs; men, women and children came and lined up before the board. A comb was put into their hair; if it fell out, they must have straight or curly hair and so one condition was fulfilled.

"How tall was your father?" a board member might ask.

"This high," an exhibit might reply. If he indicated the height by stretching out his arm in a horizontal direction, it was likely that the exhibit was "coloured"; for Africans generally indicate height by bending the arm at the elbow so that the forearm points in a vertical direction. Another condition fulfilled or found to be an obstruction.

A family woke up one morning wondering if they had been through a dream: some of its members had been declared "coloured" and others "native". But how was it possible that a whole family could experience the same dream? Once a "native", one had to carry a pass to permit one to live in an area, to enter another, to look for work in a town. It would be an indefensible criminal offence if one failed to show the pass to a policeman. Once a "native", one's wages had to be lowered.

"Look, man, T," Karel said to us one cold evening after

taking a seat in our kitchen. "I must go to that board of bastards."

He took us by surprise. He took a cup of tea from my wife and stirred it in exaggerated circular movements of his whole arm from the shoulder. He might have been paddling a canoe, with that arm that looked like a heavy club. The tea slopped over into the saucer.

"To the board? But you don't have to tell them you are a native African?"

Karel looked down.

"What de hell, no." I looked at my wife, and she looked at me.

"I told you my farder was Portugalese. Dat makes me 'coloured', *nê* ?"

"I know, but . . ." I did not know what I wanted to say.

"Look man, T, I — I can't go dress up in de watchimball, er, pass office dere for dis t'ing what you folks carry. Listen, T, I see youse folks get stopped by de bloody police day an' night: I see you folks when de whites at de post office want you to show your pass before dey give you a parcel or watchimball, er, registered letter; I see you folks in a line-up on Sunday morning when police pick you up for not havin' a pass in your pocket an' dey take you to de station. Look man, T, one night you don't come home at de time your wife's waiting to see you, eh? Now she gets frightened, she t'inks, oh, my man may be locked up. She look for de pass in de house and dere it is you forgot it. She puts on her shawl an' she takes de kids next door as' she locks up de house an' she goes to de police station. Which one? Dere's too many. She t'inks, I must go to de hospital? Maybe you's hurt or knocked down. But she's sure it must be some police station. No-one wants to ring de different stations to fin' out. Hell man, she's lost. De papers tell us all dis plenty times. Sometimes it's de last time she saw you in de morning when you goes to work. Maybe you couldn't pay your watchimball, er, admission of guilt and de police sentences you. Dere's a lorry waiting to pick up guys like you wit' no money for admission or who t'ink you'll talk for yourself in de magistrate court. A white man takes you to his farm far away from here to work like slaves. Maybe you die dere and your wife will never see your grave, T, never-never."

I was struck dumb. What argument could one have against this recital of things one knew so well? Hadn't one read these accounts in the press? Hadn't one seen and known personally families who had waited for a husband, a son, a cousin, who was never going to come? Hadn't one read these accounts in the press and felt something claw inside one's insides and creep up to the throat and descend to the lower regions until one seemed untouchably hot all over?

I ventured to say feebly, "You wouldn't be the only one, Karel. Isn't one strengthened by the fact that one is not suffering alone?"

"I ain't no coward, T. What about de wages? My wages will go down if I simply agree I'm black. Anudder 'coloured' man may push me out of dis job."

"But you *are* African, Karel. You as good as said so yourself often. You came to live with us blacks because you felt purity of blood was just lunatic nonsense, didn't you?"

"Look man, T, de word 'native' doesn't simply mean one's got black blood or African blood. It's a p'litical word, man. You's a native because you carry a pass, you can't go to watchimball, er, Parliament. You can't vote, you live in dis location. One can be proud of being an African but not a *native.*"

"What does your woman say about this, Karel?"

"Oh, you know she never says not'ing to dis'point me, T."

"But do you know what she thinks?"

"Can't say, T. Sometime she seems to say, Yes, sometime No, but she always say, Do what you think is the right thing, Karel."

My wife and I were sitting up one Saturday night when she said, "Why does the man keep talking about this like someone who cannot hold hot roasted pumpkin pips in his mouth? Why not go and get the paper to show that he has 'coloured' paint on him instead of ringing bells everywhere to tell us he wants to go!"

"No, no, Pulane, you're not being fair. As far we know, he talks to us only about it."

"*To us only, ugh!* You should hear people talk about it in the whole street."

I did not try to ascertain if she meant the whole street, but said instead, "I think he wants to be sure first he will be doing the right thing."

"*Ag*, he's just a coward, finished. Just like all 'coloureds'. Blacks are nice and good as long as a 'coloured' man is not told to become black."

"Why should anyone want to be black?"

"Isn't it that he wants to show the white people he's 'coloured'? Isn't it that he thinks we blacks are nice to live with as long as he doesn't carry a pass as we do and get the same wages as we do? See them. Paul Kruger told them they were like white people and were civilized. Now you go round this corner, 'coloured' people have better houses; you turn round that corner, 'coloured' people get better money; you go the bioscope, the 'coloured' people sit at the back and we blacks are put right in front where we can almost kiss the, er, what's its name? *Ag*, they make me feel hot between the thighs, these 'coloureds'!"

"Would you not want these good things they're getting?"

"Of course! What kind of question is that?"

"But you are not asking to be a 'coloured' woman are you?"

"*Sies*, me? Would you like to see me 'coloured'?"

"See what I mean! And you seem to want Karel to carry our burdens as a price for liking us and living with us. Who are we to say the 'coloureds' should not want to keep the good things they have?"

"I just don't want people having it both ways, that's what. They like us as people to laugh with, not to suffer with. We are the laughing, cheerful blacks, the ones full of life and entertainment, the ones they run to when they're tired of being 'coloureds', Europeans, Indians. As for the Indians, they like their curry and rice and *roti* and money and mosques and temples too much to pretend they want us for next-door neighbours. I can't blame them because they don't try to bluff anyone. Look how the Indian boys run about with 'coloured' girls! They want nothing more than to keep their business sites and help us shout from the platform. *Ag*, they all make me sick, these pinks."

She stood up and took the kettle from the stove with the force it would require if it were glued on. She filled it with water and put it back on the stove, all but throwing it down.

"And you think the Indian folk who join us in protesting are merely bluffing? And the whites, the Indians and 'coloureds' whose homes smell of police uniforms because of unending raids, and who are banned and sent to prison — are they just having a good time, just putting on a performance? Well, I don't know, child of my mother-in-law, but that is a very expensive performance and not so funny."

These had been times when I wasn't sure myself if I didn't really feel as my wife did.

After a spell of silence she got up to make tea. Meantime I went out to stand on the stoep. For some strange reason, while I looked at the blazing red sky over Iscor steel works five miles away, I thought of Karel's wife. The gentle-looking nurse who never said much any time . . .

Back inside the house, my wife said: "I wonder how much longer it is going to be for us Africans to keep making allowances and to give way to the next man to turn things round in our head, to do the explaining and to think of others' comfort."

I looked into my cup, looking for something clever to say in reply. I could not find it. But I know it had something to do with the African revolution . . .

"I got de identity card at last," Karel said casually a few months later.

"So!"

"De white trash! Dey wantin' to trap a guy all-a-time, bastards. Man, T, *hulle dink altyd hulle hol 'n mens toe* — dey t'ink dey goin' to drive me into a dead corner, sons of white bitches." He paused. "Been waiting for papers from LM. My late Ma put dem in a box and sent it to LM." He looked tired and uninterested in his achievement. His voice and posture spelled humiliation to an embarrassing degree — or was it my own embarrassment? Perhaps. I didn't have the courage to ask him to give the details of the examination which must have dragged on for a number of days with a number of breaks.

"So you'll have to leave our location and the law's going to pull you away from your wife."

"I been t'inking about dat, T. Dey can do all dey want dey'll never do buggerall to me and my woman, true's God. An' I don' take back my identity card. I stay 'coloured' and live wit' my woman."

I thought about my wife's talk about people wanting to have it both ways.

Nor did Karel make any effort to leave Corner B. But we knew that the location's white superintendent would sooner or later be sticking a rough twig between Karel's buttocks to drive him out of the location.

Meantime, Karel's right leg had begun to give him trouble. He was complaining of sleepless nights because of it. He tried to maintain an even tempo in his life, and his laugh was still loud, clear and full. Even so, in the ear of one who knew him as well as I did, it was losing its roundness and developing sharp edges. When the autumn rains came down he complained more and more. He could not pretend any longer that he did not need to limp. He visited the General Hospital times without number. He was subjected to radiography countless times. The doctors prescribed one thing after another — to drink, to massage.

"*Ag* man, T, dese white doctors are playing around wit' me now. I do everyt'in' dey tell me an' al dey do is shake de blerry head wit' sandy brains. Dey loudmout' when dey tell us dey clever educated but dey know f-all. *What can I do*, man, I ask dem. Dey'll kill me wit' dat X-ray one day."

I felt by proxy the leaping fire that must have been

scorching its way through him to release the tongue of flame that spoke these words.

One night Karel's wife came to wake me up to come to him. He wanted to see me, she said. I found him on top of his blankets, his face wet with perspiration. His wife was still fully dressed, applying a hot fomentation.

"Have you ever heard of such a miracle!" his wife said. Before I could reply she said, "Karel is talking in parables, I am sure, *hau!* He's telling me he wants to see a witch-doctor. *Hei*, people, *Modisana* !"She looked at him as if she was taking out tablets from a bottle. "Just ask him."

"Listen man, T, I'm told some of dese watchimball, er, witchdoctor guys can do it. If de white man is beaten maybe black medicine will do it, man."

"Now you're not going to do such a stupid thing," his wife said. I had never heard her speak with such authority, such a bold face. Here on the question of sickness and patients, I felt, she was sure of herself. Looking at me: "I would rather take him to another hospital far out of Pretoria, borrow money somewhere, spend all my savings to pay white doctors. Tell him, you're his friend, tell him, maybe he'll listen to you." She stooped to give him his tablets. He turned and lay on his back, with a deep round sigh.

"Listen, T, my woman here t'inks maybe I don' show t'anks for her goodness to me, for her watchimball, er, patience, for her good heart. Hang it man, T, I'm grateful from the bottom of my heart, dat's jes' why I want to make it possible for her to rest a bit. She works too hard and has to sit up de whole night a'most lookin' after me."

"What should a woman be for if she is not there to look after her man?" asked his wife.

"But — but a witchdoctor, man, Karel!" I said.

"You see him as he is," his wife said. "His boss has given him a month to stay home — on full pay you hear me? If he rests his leg for a while maybe we'll see which way we are moving. Maybe I can get a few days off to take him out to my people in the Free State. Just go away from here a bit."

"I think you should do what this good woman advises, Karel. Forget this witchdoctor madness. Besides, soon as these chaps start mucking around with one's body they're sure to meddle with parts they know nothing about."

"That is what I keep telling him, you hear."

I was less convinced about what I was saying than I may have sounded. There were always stories about someone or other who had been cured by a witchdoctor or herbalist after white doctors had failed. The performers of these wonders — as they sounded to be — were invariably said to have come from Vendaland in the farthest recesses of the rain-making queen's territory of the Northern Transvaal. Some time before this a school principal in Corner B had asked a herbalist next to his house to give him a purgative. He had almost immediately become ill and died on his way to hospital. The herbalist had been arrested, but had pleaded that he had advised the teacher to take plenty of water with and after the herb, which thing he must have failed to do. No one had seen him take the herb who could say whether he had followed the instructions or not. Most of us, whether teachers or not, whether townspeople of long standing or not, believed one way or another in ancestral spirits. The same people might at the same time tolerate the Christian faith, or even think their belief in ancestral spirits reinforced by it. How could anyone be sure? A man like Karel trying to ride a huge wave of pain:

what use was there trying to tell him not to seek help outside the hospital? What he said to me the next moment was disarming.

"Listen, T." He paused as if he had forgotten what he was going to say. "Listen, de doctor at de hospital says to me yesterday, he says I'm sure you got kaffir poison. Kaffir poison, you mean what dey call native poison? I ask. He says, Yes. I say, You can't take out kaffir poison? An' he says, No, he says, it's not for white medicine. An' again I says, What do you t'ink doctor? An' he shows me he doesn't know."

"And you think he was telling you what to do without saying so?"

"Yes, dat's not funny. You see for yourself how dese whites queue up at de African watchimball, er, herbalist's place at Selborne."

"Those are poor whites," his wife hastened to remark. "Poor, poor, poor boers or whites from cheap suburbs. What do they know better than that!" "Dey wouldn't be queueing up every day like dat if he wasn't doing dem any good." "Nonsense," was all I could say. And the cocks started to crow. Just then he dropped off to sleep. I stood up and took his wife's arm to reassure her that I was going to stay on her side.

Once again, when Karel could stand up, he walked about. He seemed to have recovered his old cheerful mood again, except for thin lines under his eyes to show that pain had kicked him about and marched through him with hobnailed boots on.

"I feel quite right now," he said to me. "Yes, a small slow pain but I t'ink it will go. I must see it goes because I'm sure de boss will not give me more days at de end of de t'irty days. Dey never do dat dese whites. Can't see myself more time in de house if I'm not getting well, and not getting paid neither."

The note of urgency in his voice told me that he must have something on his mind. What, I wondered.

"I'm goin' to watchimball, to Selborne," he said another day. "I'm takin' a bus."

Two days passed.

"*Hei wena* — You, our friend had a visitor this morning," my wife reported.

"What visitor?"

"A man with a bag in his hand. The sort you see witch-doctors carry."

"So, just at the time his wife is at work, I thought.

"Are you going to tell his woman?"

I was irritated at her use of 'you' as if to disengage herself. No, I'd go and tell him a few hard things and I'd not mince words, I told her.

I did, but he only laughed and said I shouldn't be foolish. The man knew the particular ailment he had described to him. Wasn't fussy either about the fee for opening his bag. Yes man, he had thrown the bones and shells on the floor and spoken to them and they told him how things were. Someone had smeared "some stuff" on his bicycle pedal and it had gone up his leg. Did he say the Jew boss liked him? Yes, very much. Any other black workers at the garage? Two others. Ever had a quarrel with any one of them? Now let's see. No. Was he senior to them? Yes. Some black people have clean hearts, others have black hearts. He could see the way one bone on the fringe was facing. He could hear it talk. He could see one of the garage workers going to an evil doctor to buy black magic.

"It's dere man, T, *die Here weet* — God knows."

"Do you know a saying in my language that it takes a witch to track down another?" I said.

"I don't care if dis one's a witch. It's my leg give me worryness. Man, T, you can see he can't be lying. His face, his eyes are full of wisdom. He took two days to look for de trouble, *two days*. And he talks to me nice, T, takes de trouble, not like dose white watchimballs — bastards at de hospital!"

I left him after his wife had entered.

The next day, instead of taking my sandwiches and tea in the staff-room, I cycled home in order to see how Karel was. My mind was full of ugly forebodings . . . My wife told me that she had taken him lunch as usual but found the "visitor" and so did not stay. Karel did not look worse than the previous day.

When I entered, the "visitor" was not there. But Karel was lying on the bed, his leg stretched out and resting on a tiny bench. Under the bench was a rag, saturated with blood. "What have you done, Karel!" I exclaimed.

"I feel all right, T. De leg will be all right from now. The man dug a hole in the ankle for the poison to come out. Ah!" He released a long heavy sigh. He held his hip with his still-powerful hand, and let it slide down his side, thigh and leg, like one pressing something out of a tube. At the same time he screwed up his face to show how much energy he was putting into the act.

"Ah, T," came the long long sigh again, "I can feel de watchimball — de pain moving out of the hole there. The blood is carrying it out. Oh, shit!" After a pause, he said, "A black man like you, T, can go a long way. A black man has people around him to give him strength. I haven't."

The facial muscles relaxed and his arm hung limp at his side. I looked at the ankle more carefully this time, as much as I dared. The sight of the blood oozing out like that from the inside part of the ankle, and the soaking wet rag on the floor shocked me out of my stupor and confusion. I looked around for a cloth, found one and bandaged the ankle. Without a word, I ran out to my house. I scribbled a note to my headmaster and asked my wife to go and watch over Karel while I went for a doctor a few streets up. He was out making home visits together with his nurse. I was frantic. Move him to hospital twelve miles away? The white hospital four miles away would not touch him. What about transport? Go to the location superintendent to ring the hospital? I gave up. I left a note for the doctor. I went back to wait.

Death came and took him away from us.

While I was helping to clear things up in the house, several days later when Karel's wife was permitted by custom to reorganize their home, she said to me: "I believe Karel once told you about his identity card?" "Yes." She held it in her hand. "I don't know if I should keep it."

My thinking machine seemed to have come to a dead stop and I couldn't utter a word.

"*Ag*, what use is it?" she said.

"Can I see it please?"

Below his picture appeared many other bits of information:

NAME: KAREL BENITO ALMEIDA

RACE: COLOURED

I gave it back. She tore it to bits.

"Did he tell you about this letter?" She handed it over to me.

It was a letter from the location's white superintendent telling Karel that he would have to leave house No. 35 Mathole Street where he was known to live, and was forbidden from occupying any other house in Corner B as he was registered "coloured" and should not be in a "Bantu location".

She took the letter and tore it to bits.

"Soon I know I must leave this house."

"Why? You can tell the superintendent that you are his widow. I know widows are always ejected soon as their men are under the ground. We can help you fight it out." But I knew this was useless heroic talk: the law of the jungle always wins in the end. But that is another story. And in any case, "I was not married to Karel by law," the good woman said.

Grieg on a Stolen Piano

Those were the days of terror when, at the age of 15, he ran away from home and made his way towards Pietersburg town. Driven by hunger and loneliness and fear he took up employment on an Afrikaner's farm at ten shillings a month plus salted mealie-meal porridge and an occasional piece of meat. There were the long scorching hours when a posse of horsemen looked for him and three other labourers while they were trying to escape. The next morning at dawn the white men caught up with them.

Those were the savage days when the whole white family came and sat on the stoep to watch, for their own amusement, African labourers put under the whip. Whack! Whack! Whack! And while the leather whip was still in the air for the fourth stroke on the buttocks, he yelled, *ma-oeeee!* As the arm came down, he flew up from the crude bench he was lying on, and, in a manner that he could never explain afterwards, hooked the white foreman's arm with his two, so that for a few seconds he dangled a few feet from the ground. Amid peals of laughter from the small pavilion, the foreman shook him off as a man does a disgusting insect that creeps on his arm.

Those were the days when, in a solo flight again towards Pietersburg, terror clawed at his heart as he travelled through thick bush. He remembered the stories he had so often listened to at the communal fireplace; tales of huge snakes that chased a man on the ground or leapt from tree to tree; tales of the giant snake that came to the river at night to drink, breaking trees in its path, and before which helpless people lay flat on their stomachs wherever they might be at the time; none dared to move as the snake mercifully lifted its body above them, bent over, drank water and then, mercifully again, turned over backwards, belly facing upwards, rolling away from the people; stories that explained many mysteries, like the reason why the owl and the bat moved in the dark. Always the theme was that of man, helpless as he himself was in the bush or on a tree or in a rock cave on a hill, who was unable to ward off danger, to escape a terrible power that was everywhere around him. Something seemed to be stalking him all the time, waiting for the proper moment to pounce on him.

But he walked on, begged and stole food and got lifts on lorries, until he reached Thswane — Pretoria.

There was the brief time in "the kitchens", as houses of white people are called where one does domestic work, as if the white suburbs were simply a collection of kitchens. There were the brutal Sundays when he joined the Pietersburg youth, then working in the kitchens, on their wild march to the open ground just outside Bantule location for the sport of bare fisticuffs. They marched in white shorts on broad slabs of feet in tennis shoes and vaseline-smeared legs: now crouching, now straightening up, now wielding their fists wrapped in white hand- kerchiefs. One handkerchief dangled out of a trouser pocket, just for show. The brutal fisticuffs, mouths flushed with blood; then the white mounted police who herded them back to the kitchens; the stampede of horses' hooves as the police chased after them, for fun . . .

Those were the days when chance like a crane lifted him out of the kitchens and out of the boxing arena, and deposited him in Silverton location. This was when his aunt, having been alerted by her brother, had tracked him down.

There was regular schooling again. At twenty he began teacher-training at Kilnerton Institution nearby. There were the teaching days, during which he studied privately for a junior secondary school certificate.

Those were the days, when, as the first black man in the province to write an examination for a certificate, he timidly entered a government office for the first paper. The whites stared at him until he had disappeared into the room where he would write in isolation. And those were the days when a black man had to take off his hat as soon as he saw a white man approach, when the black man had to keep clear of street pavements.

Then the return home — the first time in seven years — as a hero, a teacher. The parents bubbled over with pride. Then the feast . . .

It was one of those hot subtropical nights when Pretoria seems to lie in its valley, battered to insensibility by the day's heat, the night when a great friend of his was tarred and feathered by white students of the local university at Church Square: Mr Lambeth, a British musician who had come to teach at Kilnerton where he discovered this black young man's musical talent. He had given his time free to teach him the piano. Many were the afternoons, the nights, the weekends that followed of intensive, untiring work at the instrument. What else had Mr Lambeth done wrong, he asked himself several times after the incident. The Englishman had many friends among African teachers whom he visited in their locations; he adjudicated at their music competitions.

This black young man was my uncle. He was actually a cousin of my late father's. So, according to custom, my father had referred to him as "my brother". As my father had no blood brothers, I was glad to avail myself of an uncle. When my father died, he charged my uncle with the responsibility of "helping me to become a man". It meant that I had someone nearby who would give me advice on a number of things concerned with the problem of growing up. My mother had died shortly afterwards. Uncle has seven children, all but one of whom are earning their living independently. The last-born is still in school.

Uncle is black as a train engine; so black that his face often gives the illusion of being blueish. His gums are a deep red which blazes forth when he smiles, overwhelming the dull rusty colour of his teeth. He is tall and walks upright. His head is always close-shaven because, at sixty, he thinks he is prematurely greying, although his hair began to show grey at thirty. He keeps his head completely bald because he does not want a single grey hair to show.

His blackness has often led him into big-big trouble with the whites, as he often tells us.

"*Hei! Jy!* "

Uncle walks straight on, pretending not to see the bunch of them leaning against a fence. He is with a friend, a classmate.

"*Hei! Jy! Die pikswart een, die bobbejaan!* " — the pitch-black one, the baboon.

One of them comes towards the two and pushes his way

between them, standing in front. They stop dead.

A juvenile guffaw behind him sends a shiver through uncle. He breaks through his timidity and lunges at the white boy. He pummels him. In Pietersburg boxing style he sends the boy down with a knee that gets him in a strategic place on the jaw. The others are soon upon them. The Africans take to their heels . . .

A new white clerk is busy arranging postal orders and recoding them. The queue stretches out, out of the post office building. The people are making a number of clicking noises to indicate their impatience. They crane their necks or step out of the queue in order to see what is happening at the counter.

Uncle is at the head of the queue.

"Excuse me," he ventures, "playtime will soon be over and my class will be waiting for me, can you serve us, please?"

The clerk raises his head.

"Look here," he says aggressively, "I'm not only here to serve kaffirs, I'm here to work!"

Uncle looks at him steadily. The clerk goes back to his postal orders. After about fifteen minutes he leaves them. He goes to a cupboard and all the eyes in the queue follow each movement of his. When he comes back to the counter, he looks at the man at the head of the queue, who in turn fixes his stare on him. The white man seems to recoil at the sight of Uncle's face. Then, as if to fall back on the last mode of defence, he shouts, "What are you? What are you? — Just a black kaffir, a kaffir monkey, black as tar. Now any more from you and I'll bloody well refuse to serve the whole bloody lot of you. Teacher — teacher, teacher *te hel!* "

Irritation and impatience can be heard to hiss and sigh down the queue.

Uncle realizes he's been driven into a corner and wonders if he can contain the situation. Something tells him it is beyond him. The supervisor of post comes in just then, evidently called in by his junior's shout.

"*Ja?*" he asks, "*wat is dit?*"

"Your clerk has been insulting me — calling me a kaffir monkey."

The clerk opens his mouth to speak, but his superior leads him round a cubicle. After a few moments, the clerk comes back, ready to serve but sulky, and mute.

Uncle says that, throughout, the white clerk seemed to feel insulted at the sudden confrontation with such articulate human blackness as thrust itself forward through the wire mesh of the counter.

This time, Uncle had the satisfaction of causing the removal of the white clerk after a colleague, who had been an eye witness of the incident in the post office, had obtained support from fellow teachers at Silverton to petition a higher postal authority against the clerk.

"Can you see that happening today?" he asked. "No, man, I'd have been fired at once on a mere allegation out of the clerk's important mouth."

Years later, Uncle was promoted to the post of junior inspector of African schools (the white man always senior). He went to live in the Western Transvaal. This is where his wife died while giving birth. He really hit the bottom of depression after this. The affection he had for his wife found a perverse expression in drink and he took to his music with a deeper and savage passion which, as he puts it, was a kind of hot fomentation to help burst the boil of grief inside him. He kept his children with him, though.

Each one had the opportunity to go to an institution of higher education. Here he was lucky. For although all of them were mediocre, they used what they had profitably and efficiently. One did a degree in science; another played the saxophone in a band; another was a teacher and "pop singer"; another became a librarian for an institute of research into race relations; one daughter went in for nursing, and a son and a daughter were still in secondary school.

There were nights of sheer terror when their father failed to return home, and they knew he must be in some drinking orgy somewhere. Then they got to know that he was doing illicit diamond-buying. As he visited schools in his circuit, he sold or bought small stones. But he was always skating near the edge. Once he had the bitter experience of discovering that he had bought a few fakes for £50 from an African agent.

Then there was the day he says he'll never forget as long as he lives. The CID, after crossing his path several times and picking up and losing trails, finally came to the converging point — Uncle. They found him in a train from Johannesburg to Kimberley. They took him to the luggage van and questioned him. Nothing was found on him, and he wouldn't talk. When eventually they realized they might have a corpse on their hands, they put him out on a station platform, battered, bleeding and dazed. His suitcase was thrown in his direction.

Uncle was transferred to Johannesburg, but not without incident. A white educational officer wanted him to carry his typewriter — a heavy table model — to his car outside. Uncle told him he wouldn't. He had, before this, refused to wash the official's car when asked to do so. As the educational authorities had a high opinion of his work after several years in the department, they engineered a transfer for him. If you ask him how he managed to keep his post, he will tell you, "I made more or less sure I didn't slip up that side, and besides whites don't like a correct black man, because they are so corrupt themselves."

Each time after some verbal tiff with a white man, Uncle says, he felt his extra blackness must have been regarded as an insult by those who found themselves in the shadow it seemed to cast around him.

His arrival in Johannesburg was like surfacing. He went slow on his drink, and even became a lay preacher in the Methodist Church at Orlando. But he started to go to the races, and threw himself into this kind of gambling with such passion that he resigned as preacher.

"I can't keep up the lies," he said. "There are people who can mix religion with gambling and the other things, but I can't. And gamble I must. As Christ never explained what a black man should do in order to earn a decent living in this country, we can only follow our instincts. And if I cannot understand the connection, it is not right for me to stand in the pulpit and pretend to know the answer."

The "other things" were illicit diamond dealing and trading as a travelling salesman, buying and selling soft goods, mostly stolen by some African gang or other that operated in the city. There were also workers who systematically stole articles from their employers' shops and sold them to suburban domestic servants and location customers. While he was visiting schools, he would call this man and that man round the corner or into some private room to do business.

Uncle married again. He was now living with three of his

children, two of whom were still in secondary school. A cloud descended upon his life again. His wife was an unpleasant, sour woman. But Uncle woke up to it too late. She sat on the stoep like a dumpling and said little beyond smiling briefly a word of greeting and giving concise answers to questions. The children could not quarrel with her, because she said little that could offend anyone. But her antheap appearance was most irritating, because she invited no-one's cooperation and gave none beyond fulfilling the routine duties of a wife. She did not seem to like mothering anyone.

Once she succeeded, perhaps in all innocence, in raising a furore in the house.

"You must find out more about the choir practice your daughter keeps going to every week," she says to Uncle in the presence of the other children. They had stopped calling her "Ma" because she insisted on referring to them as "your daughter" or "your son" when she talked to their father about them.

"It's choir practice," Uncle said brusquely.

"*Wai-i-i!* I know much about choir practices, me. A man's daughter can go to them without stopping and one-two-three the next time you look at her she has a big choir practice in her stomach."

The girl ran into her bedroom, crying. Soon tongues were let loose upon her. But she continued to sit like an antheap, her large body seeming to spread wider and wider like an overgrown pumpkin. Her attitude seemed to suggest much Uncle would have liked to know. What *was* she hiding?

"What do you do with such a woman?" Uncle sighed when he told me about the incident.

He was prepared to go through with the "companion-ship", to live with her to the end of his days. "I promised I'd do so in church," he remarked. "And I was in my full senses, no-one forced me into the thing."

Another time he threatened, "One day I'll get so angry, neph', I'll send her away to her people. And at her station I'll put her on a wheelbarrow like a sack of mealies and wheel her right into her people's house if I've to bind her with a rope."

I knew he was never going to do it.

Uncle could only take dramatic decisions which were not going to leave him any need to exercise responsibility either to revoke them or fall back on them. He made decisions as a man makes a gamble: once made, you won or lost, and the matter rested there. It was the same with his second marriage, I think. He met the woman during a church conference when he was by chance accommodated in her house in Randfontein together with two other delegates, according to the arrangement of the local branch. His wife had been dead twelve years. He had decided that his children were big enough not to look so helpless if a second marriage soured the home atmosphere by any chance. His personal Christian belief would not permit him to get out of a marriage contract. This was the kind of responsibility he would want to avoid. If there was a likely chance that he might have to decide to revoke a step later, he did not take it.

There was in Uncle a synthesis of the traditional and the westernized African. At various periods in his life he felt that ill-luck was stalking him, because misfortune seemed to pour down on him in torrents, particularly in money matters, family relations, and relations with white educational authorities. At times like these, Uncle went and bought a goat, slaughtered it, and called relations to come and eat the meat and mealie-meal porridge with their bare hands, sitting on the floor. He then buried the bones in the yard. At such times his mind searched the mystery of fate, groping in some imagined world where the spirits of his ancestors and that of his dead wife must be living, for a point of contact, for a line of communication.

After the feast, he felt peace settle inside him and fill his whole being until it seemed to ooze from the pores of his body as the tensions in him thawed . . . Then he would face the world with renewed courage or with the reinforced, secure knowledge that he was at peace with his relations, without whom he considered he would be a nonentity, a withered twig that has broken off from its tree.

Twice when I was ill, Uncle called in an African medical doctor. But when my migraine began and often seemed to hurl me into the den of a savage beast, he called in an African herbalist and witchdoctor. The man said he could divine from his bones that I had once — it didn't matter when or where — inhaled fumes that had been meant to drive me insane, prepared by an enemy. So he in turn burned a few sticks of a herb and made me inhale the smoke. It shot up my nasal cavity, hit the back of my skull, seeming to scrape or burn its path from the forehead to the nape of my neck. Each time, after repeated refusals to be seen by a medicine man, my resistance broke down. I felt temporary relief each time.

So he was going to keep his wife, rain or shine. When her behaviour or her sullenness depressed him, he went back to his whisky. Then he played excerpts from Grieg's piano concerto or a Chopin nocturne, or his own arrangements of Mohapeloa's *Chuchu-makhala* (*The Train*) or *Leba* (*The Dove*) and others, vocalizing passages the while with his deep voice. He loved to evoke from his instrument the sound of the train's siren *Oi-oi-i-i* while he puffed *Chu-chu, chu-chu.*

"If she knew this piano was lifted out of a shop," he thought aloud often, "this dumpling would just let off steam about the fact, simply to annoy me, to make me feel I'm a failure because she knows I'm not a failure and she wants to eat me up and swallow me up raw the way she did her first husband."

He had lately disposed of his twenty-year-old piano.

The keyboards felt the impact of these passionate moments and resounded plaintively and savagely. Self-pity, defiance, contempt, endurance, all these and others played musical chairs in his being.

"Look neph'," Uncle said one day when he was his cheerful, exuberant self again, "look, here's an advertisement for an African beauty contest in *Afric.*"

"Oh, there is such a rash of beauty contests we're all sick of them. It's the racket in every big town these days. Haven't they learned that a woman is as beautiful as your eyes make her?"

"You're just too educated, that's all. You know nothing, my boy, wait till I tell you."

"Is it a new money-catching thing again? Don't tell me you're going to run a gambling game around the winning number?"

Uncle and beauty queens simply did not dovetail in my mind. What was behind that volume of blackness that frightened so many whites? I was curious to know.

"Better than that, neph'. If you want to cooperate."

"In what?"

"Now look at the prizes: £500, £250, £150 and consolation prizes. One of these can be ours."

"But this is a beauty contest, not a muscle show."

"Don't be so stupid. Now, here. I know a lovely girl we can enter for this contest."

I felt my curiosity petering out.

"I go and fetch the girl — she's a friend's daughter living in the Western Transvaal, in a village. Just the right kind of body, face, but she needs to be brought up to market standard. The contest is nine months away still, and we've time."

"But — "

"Now listen. You put in £25, me the same. We can then keep the girl in my house — no, your aunt will curdle again — now let me think — yes, in my friend Tau's house; his wife has a beautiful heart. The money will go to feeding her and paying for her lessons at Joe's gym. Your job will be to take her out, teach her how to smile when she's introduced; how to sit — not like an Afrikaner cow. You've got to cultivate in her a sense of public attention. Leave the body work to Joe. If she wins, we give her £100, and split £400."

Joe was one of those people who knows just when to come in for profit. He sets up his gym in a hired hall with the express aim of putting candidates through "body work".

For my part, I simply did not like the idea at all. Beauty on a platform: beauty advertised, beauty mixed up with money; that is how the thing seemed to me, a person with the simple tastes of a lawyer's clerk. To what extent Uncle had assimilated jazzy urban habits, I couldn't tell.

"Thought about it yet, neph'? We can't wait too long, you know."

"Yes, Unc', but I just don't see the point of it. Why don't we leave the beauty queens to the — er — experts?" I actually meant something much lower than experts. "Like Joe, for instance."

"Joe's just a spiv," Uncle replied. "He just loves to rub shoulders with top dogs, that's all. We are investing."

"But I've only £30 in the post office savings; if I take out £25, I shall be almost completely out."

"A black man never starves if he lives among his people, unless there is famine. If the worst comes to the worst, you would have to be content with simply having food, a roof over your head, and clothing."

"That's rural thinking. The extra things a man wants in the city I can't afford."

"Two hundred pounds can give you the extras."

I paused to think.

"No, Unc', gambling is for the rich, for those who can afford to lose, not for people like us."

"You think I'm rich? Don't be silly, you mean to say all those hunch-backed, dried-up, yellow-coloured whites you see at the races and betting booths are rich?"

I relented after a good deal of badgering. Who knows, I thought, we may just win. What couldn't I do with £200 if it came to me!

What a girl!

Her face was well shaped all right: every feature of it was in place, although she had a dry mouth and an unpleasant complexion. She could not have been well in the Western Transvaal. Her bones stuck out at the elbows, and her buttocks needed filling out.

"What is your name?" I asked her.

"Tryphina." I almost giggled, thinking: what names some people have!

"That name won't do, Unc'," I said to him at the house, affecting a touch of showmanship. "I can't imagine the name coming out of the mouth of the MC when he calls it out."

"Call her 'Try' or 'Tryph'," he said indifferently.

"No, they sound like syllables in a kindergarten reading class. Just as bad as 'Jenina' or 'Judida' or 'Hermina' or 'Stephina'."

"Let's use her Sesotho name; she should have one I'm sure."

"Torofina," she said. "No, not the school name spoken in Sesotho, I mean your real Sotho name. You see, in things like a beauty competition, people like an easy name that is smooth on the tongue (I meant *sweet to the ear*). They may even fail you for having a difficult name."

Didn't I loathe *Afric*'s cheap, slick, noisy journalism.

"Oh, Kefahliloe," she said sweetly, which means "something has got into my eye". "That is what they call me at home."

"Nice," I commented, meaning nothing of the sort. "But you don't have a shorter Sesotho name?"

"No." She was still all innocence and patience.

"Well — er — maybe you can — er — think of an English name. Just for the contest, you see, and for the newspapers and magazines. Your picture is going to appear in all the papers. We'll call you Kefahliloe — a person's name is her name, and there's nothing wrong in it. Do not hurry, you can tell us the name you've chosen later. Is it all right?" She nodded. Things never seemed all wrong with her. Sometimes there was something pathetic about her pliability, sometimes something irritating.

The next day she gave it to us, with a take-it-or-leave-it tone: Mary-Jane.

The first three months showed a slight improvement. Her weight was going up, her paleness was disappearing, the lips moistening and softening, her small eyes taking on a new liveliness and self-confidence. Joe was doing the body work efficiently. I felt then, and Uncle agreed, like one who had known it all along, that there was something latent in the girl which we were going to draw out in the next few months.

She had finished her primary schooling and done part of secondary school, so she was all right on that side.

I took her to the bioscope on certain Saturdays, especially to musicals, which appealed to her more than straight drama or bang-bang movies. I took her to Dorkay House in Eloff Street where African musicians go each Saturday for jazz improvisations. There we found other boys and girls listening eagerly, ripples of excitement visibly travelling through the audience as now and again they whistled and clapped hands. The girls were the type called in township slang "rubbernecks", the ostentatiously jazzy type. We found the same type at parties.

Mary-Jane was drinking it all in, I noticed.

I invited her to my room to listen to my collection of jazz records. She took in small doses at a time, and seemed to digest it; her bodily movements were taking on a city rhythm.

Uncle and I shared entertainment expenses equally. We went for cheap but good entertainment.

After six months, Uncle and I knew we were going to

deliver a presentable article of good healthy flesh, comportment, and luscious charm. Charm? Strange. Through all this I did not notice the transformation that was taking place in this direction. She was close on twenty-one, and at the end of those six months, I was struck by the charm that was creeping out of her, seeming to wait for a time, far off, when it would burst into blossom. She was filling out, but her weight was in no danger of overshooting the mark. Her tongue was loosening up.

I was becoming aware of myself. I felt a twinge of guilt at treating her like an article that should be ready against a deadline. Before I could realize fully what was happening, the storm had set in. The thing was too delicate; I would have to go about it carefully. Particularly so because I had sensed that she was innocent and untutored in a rustic manner about things like love. And one didn't want the bird to take fright because one had dived into the bush instead of carefully burrowing in. Besides, I am a timid fellow, not unlike my uncle in other things.

Uncle had expensive photographs taken of Mary-Jane for the press. Publicity blazed across the African newspapers, and the air was thick with talk about *Afric* 's beauty contest at which Miss Johannesburg would be selected. "Who was going to be the 500-pound consignment of beauty dynamite?" the journal screamed . . .

I heard a snatch of conversation in the train one morning amid the continuous din of talking voices, peals of laughter and door-slamming.

"Hey man, see dat girl's picture in *Afric* ?"

"Which?"

"De one called Mary-Jen — er — Tumelo?"

"Ja-man, Jesus, she's reely top, eh!"

"God, de body, hmm, de curves, de waist, dis t'ings!" (indicating the area of the breasts).

"*Ag* man, dat's number one, true's God jealous down."

I warmed up towards the boys and wished they would continue.

"I've seen the three judges," Uncle said.

"The judges? But *Afric* hasn't published the names!"

"They don't *do* such things, you backward boy."

"How did you know them?"

"I've my contacts."

"But we don't do such things, Uncle!" I gasped.

"What things?"

"Talking to judges about a competition in which you have vested interests."

"Don't talk so pompously. You're talking English. Let's talk Sesotho. Now all I did is I took photographs of Mary-Jane to each one at his house, paid my respects with a bottle of whisky and asked them if they didn't think she's a beautiful girl. What's wrong with just talking?"

"What did they think?"

"What are you talking, neph'! Each one almost jumped out of his pants with excitement."

I wanted badly to laugh, but wanted also to show him that I disapproved.

"I didn't suggest anything to them. I just said she is my niece and I was proud to see her entering the contest. They swore they hadn't seen such a beauty so well photographed among all the pictures they had seen in the papers. We're near the winning post, neph', I can see the other side of September the fifteenth already — it's bright. Those judges caught my hint."

I continued to sit with my eyes fixed on the floor, wondering whether I should feel happy or alarmed.

"By the way, neph', do you realize you have got yourself a wife, home-grown and fresh? Anything going on between you two?"

"What do you mean?" I asked without wanting to answer. His eyes told me he wasn't impressed by my affectation. He waited for me to crawl out of it.

"I haven't thought of it," I lied. After a pause, "Was this also on your mind when you thought of her as a beauty queen, Uncle?"

"Yes, neph'. I got to liking her very much while I visited her people during my inspection trips. I was sad to think that such a bright pretty girl would merely become another villager's wife and join the rest who are scratching the soil like chickens for what food there still remains in those desolate places. Her father and me are like twin brothers, we were at school together."

"But the contest? Surely you could obtain a husband for her without it? And you're not sure she'll win, either."

He was silent.

"Nor are we sure she'll like me for a husband."

"Her father knows my plans. He has told her since she came here."

"But the contest, why that?"

Silence.

"It's too difficult to explain. All I ask you is to trust me enough to know that I'm not simply playing a game with Mary-Jane for my own amusement."

During the next few days vanity blew me up. I abstracted the whole sequence of events from their setting and the characters who acted them out. Gradually I built up a picture of myself as someone who needs to be independent and around whom a hedge was being set up, the victim of a plot. I regarded myself as a sophisticate who couldn't willingly let others choose a sweetheart or wife for me. But in fact I sensed that the reason for my resentment was that I was actually in love with Mary-Jane but could not face the prospect of living with someone I had presumed to raise to a level of sophistication for reasons of money. I had often been moved by films in which the hero eventually married the less-privileged, artless and modest girls rather than the articulate, urbanized girl who goes out to get her man. Now I had the opportunity of doing the same thing, and I couldn't. In either case, I realize now, one saw a different version of male vanity at work.

Another disturbing element was my uncle's motive for doing what he did by throwing Mary-Jane into a beauty contest when he could arrive at his other objective without going into all the trouble. Although he declined to say it, I think it was his gambling urge that pushed him to it. I wondered what Mary-Jane herself thought about all this: the manner in which she was simply brought to the city and put through a machine to prepare her for a beauty competition, probably without her opinion being asked. Did she perhaps take it that this was how townspeople did things, or one of the things country people were bound to do when they came to the city? I still wonder.

Mary-Jane had to enter the competition, in spite of our vanities. She looked forward to it with zest and a certain vivacity which one would not have guessed she was capable of about nine months before. Yes, she was charming, too. How I wished I had found her like this or had arrived at it through someone else's efforts and planning!

Uncle himself infected me with his high spirits. We decided to have an Indian dinner at the Crescent, after the event.

That night came.

The lights went on full beam, washing out every bit of shade from every corner of the hall. The Jazz Dazzlers struck up "September in the Rain". Masses of faces in the packed hall looked up towards the rostrum. The music stopped. The MC's voice cut through the noise in the hall and the people held their breaths, unfinished words and sentences trailing off in a sigh.

It came to me with a metallic mockery — the announcement that *Afric* had decided that this was going to be a you-pick-the-winner show. The queen and the other two prize winners would be chosen by popular vote. There was hilarious applause and whistling from the crowd of what must have been about two thousand people. The MC explained that as the people filed out of the hall after the contest, each person would, in the presence of supervisors at the door, drop two tickets into a box fixed at every one of the four exits. One ticket would bear the numbers of the winners of the three prizes in evening dress, and the other the numbers of the winners in beach attire. The categories were indicated on the cards. Then pencils were distributed, while the band played.

I looked at Uncle next to me. I could see he was furious. He kept saying, "Stupid! Hoodlums! Cheats! Burn the bloody *Afric!* Nothing ever goes right in things organized by the Press. You take my word for it, neph'. Ah!"

"Anything happens in beauty competitions," I said, for lack of a stronger remark to match my sagging mood.

"Anyway, neph'," Uncle said, his face cheering up, "two

thousand people looking with two eyes each must be better than three men looking with two eyes each, with the possibility of a squint in one of them."

This really tickled me, in spite of myself. It gave me hope: how could one be sure that all three judges knew a lovely bust from the back of a bus or a bag of mealies? We could at least enjoy our Indian dinner and leave the rest in the hands of fate.

What use would it be to describe Mary-Jane's superb performance?

We had couples — friends — with us at dinner. Mary-Jane was most relaxed. Her ingenuous abandon and air of self-assurance went to my head. The dinner proved worth waiting for. That went to my stomach and made me feel what a glorious thing it is to have a healthy receptacle for such exquisite food.

During our 12-mile trip by car to Orlando, I felt the warm plush body of Mary-Jane press against me slightly, and I was glad to have things in contact like that. She, in turn, seemed to respond to something of what was radiating from me.

"Are you worried about the results?" I ventured to ask, merely for the sake of saying something to relieve the drowsy, full-bellied silence in the car.

"No," she replied warmly. "But I'm glad it's all over."

We lost.

Mary-Jane wasn't in the least worried. Uncle regarded it simply as a match that was lost and couldn't be replayed. For my part, I suspected that I had often heard a faint whisper within me telling me that I should be better off if we lost. So I did not know what I ought to feel.

On a Sunday I went to Uncle's house for a casual visit. I found his wife in one of her sour moods. She greeted me with the impatience of one who waves off a fly that hovers over the face and hinders conversation. She was actually talking alone, in a querulous mood. Her right elbow was resting on her huge breast and in the cup of her left hand, the right hand stroking her cheek and nose.

I passed hastily on to the room where Uncle played and sang an excerpt from Grieg's piano concerto. He saw me as I went to seat myself, but continued to play. At the end of the passage he said, casually, "She is gone," and continued playing. I shrugged my shoulders, thinking, "That is beyond me."

"She left me a note," he said. "Did you receive one?"

His eyes told me that he had just visited his whisky cupboard. I realized that he wasn't talking about his wife.

"Who? Are you talking about Mary-Jane?"

He nodded. "Who do you think I mean — Vasco da Gama's daughter-in-law?" Then he shouted, "*Ja*. Gone. With Joe!"

He went back to some crescendo passages of Grieg, picking them up and dropping them in turn. Then he suddenly stopped and came to sit by me.

"How's everybody in the house?" I asked.

"Still well. Except your aunt. That stupid native boy who sold me this piano comes here and finds your aunt and tells her this is a stolen piano. Just showing off, the clever fool. *Setlatla sa mafelelo* — fool of the first order. His mother never taught him not to confide everything in woman. Kind of lesson you suck from your mother's breast. The native! Now your aunt thinks all the house money goes out for the piano. Nothing can convince her that I'm paying £30 only, and in bits too. So, you see, she's staging one of her boycotts."

Uncle did not even pretend to lower his voice. Has it gone this far — no bother about what she thinks? I asked myself. No, he did care. He was too sensitive not to care. Always, when he told me about her, he spoke with a sense of hurt. Not such as a henpecked husband displays: Uncle had tremendous inner resources and plenty of diversions and could not buckle up under his wife's policy of non-collaboration, the way a henpecked man would do. This "speaking up" was just a bit of defiance.

"She worries about a stolen piano," Uncle continued, lying back on the divan, his eyes looking at the ceiling, his thumb playing up and down under his braces. "She forgets she sleeps between stolen sheets; every bit of cutlery that goes into her mouth was stolen by the boys from whom I bought it; her blouses are stolen goods, her stockings." And then, looking at me he said, "Don't we steal from each other, lie to each other every day and know it, us and the whites?"

I said, "*Ja,*" and looked at my tie and shoes. But I considered this superfluous explanation.

"You know, neph'," he continued in rambling fashion, "a few days ago I had a sickening experience involving a school I've been inspecting. A colleague of mine — let's call him JM — has been visiting the school for oral tests. At no time when his white superior calls him or asks him a question does JM fail to say, 'Yes, *baas,*' or 'No, *baas,*' or 'I'll get it for you, *baas.*' Now during the lunch break, some of the staff say to him in the staffroom they feel disgraced when a black man like him says '*baas, baas*' to the white man. They say they hope he'll stop it — just a nice brotherly talk, you see. Guess what JM goes and does? He goes and tells his white superior that the staff members of such-and-such a school don't want to call him '*baas*'! Guess what the white man does? He comes and complains to me about the bad conduct of those teachers. Now I ask you, what chance do you or I stand against idiots like these two who have so much power? We don't all have the liver to join the Congress Movement. So we keep stealing from the white man and lying to him and he does the same. This way we can still feel some pride."

As I rose to go, I said: "So Mary-Jane's gone off with Joe, eh!" as though her image had not been hovering over me all the time since Uncle had announced her "flight".

"Yes, because I've a stupid timid nephew. Are you going to wait till horns grow on your head before you marry?"

I laughed.

"Any country girl who starts off with Joe has made a real start in town living, neph!"

As I went out, the woman in the lounge was saying: "Kiriki, Kiriki — who do they say he is? — Kiriki with the stolen piano. Me, I cannot eat Kiriki, I want money for food. He can take that Kirikinyana and Mohapeloanyana of his, put them in the lavatory bucket."

By saying "He can take . . .", she showed she wanted me to listen. The use of the diminutive form for the names of the musicians was meant for his ears.

"What do you do with your aunt, neph', if she does not understand Grieg and cannot like Mohapeloa?"

If you had pricked me with a pin as I was going out, I should have punctured, letting out a loud bawl of laughter which I could hardly keep back in my stomach.

In Corner B

How can boys just stick a knife into someone's man like that? Talita mused. Leap out of the dark and start beating up a man and then drive a knife into him. What do the parents of such boys think of them? What does it matter now? I'm sitting in this room weeping till my heart wants to burst . . .

Talita's man was at the government mortuary, and she sat waiting, waiting and thinking in her house. A number of stab wounds had done the job, but it wasn't till he had lain in hospital for a few hours that the system caved in and he turned his back on his people, as they say. This was a Thursday. But if one dies in the middle of the week, the customary thing is to wait for a week and be buried at the first weekend after seven days. A burial must be on a weekend to give as many people as possible an opportunity to attend it. At least a week must be allowed for the next-of-kin to come from the farthest parts of the country.

There are a number of things city folk can afford to do precipitately: a couple may marry by special licence and listen to enquiries from their next-of-kin after the fact; they can be precipitate in making children and marry after the event; children will break with their parents and lose themselves in other townships; many people do not hold coming-out parties to celebrate the last day of a new-born baby's month-long confinement in the house. But death humbles the most unconventional, the hardest rebel. The dead person cannot simply be packed off to the cemetery. You are a person because of other human beings, you are told. The aunt from a distant province will never forgive you if she arrives and finds the deceased buried before she has seen his lifeless face for the last time. Between the death and the funeral, while the body lies in the mortuary (which has to be paid for) there is a wake each night. Day and night relatives and friends and their relatives and their friends come and go, saying words of consolation to the bereaved. And all the time some next-of-kin must act as spokesman to relate the circumstances of death to all who arrive for the first time. Petty intrigues and dramatic scenes among the relatives as they prepare for the funeral are innumerable. Without them, a funeral doesn't look like one.

Talita slept where she sat, on a mattress spread out on the floor in a corner, thinking and saying little, and then only when asked questions like: "What will you eat now?" or "Has your headache stopped today?" or "Are your bowels moving properly?" or "The burial society wants your marriage certificate, where do you keep it?" Apart from this, she sat or lay down and thought.

Her man was tall, not very handsome, but lovable; an insurance agent who moved about in a car. Most others in the business walked from house to house and used buses and electric trains between townships. But her man's firm was prosperous and after his fifteen years' good service it put a new car at his disposal. Merman had soft, gentle eyes and was not at all as vivacious as she. Talita often teased him about his shyness and what she called the weariness in his tongue because he spoke little. But she always prattled on and on, hardly ever short of topics to talk about.

"Ah, you met your match last night, mother-of-Luka," her man would say, teasingly.

"My what — who?"

"The woman we met at the dance and talked as if you were not there."

"How was she my match?"

"Don't pretend to be foolish — *hau*, here's a woman! She talked you to a standstill and left you almost wide-mouthed when I rescued you. Anyone who can do that takes the flag."

"*Ag*, get away! And anyhow if I don't talk enough my tongue will rot and grow mouldy."

They had lived through nineteen years of married life that yielded three children and countless bright and cloudy days. It was blissful generally, in spite of the physical and mental violence around them; the privation; police raids; political strikes and attendant clashes between the police and boycotters; death; ten years of low wages during which she experienced a long spell of ill health. But like everybody else Talita and her man stuck it through. They were in an urban township and like everybody else they made their home there. In the midst of all these living conditions, at once in spite of and because of them, the people of Corner B alternately clung together desperately and fell away from the centre; like birds that scatter when the tree on which they have gathered is shaken. And yet for each individual life, a new day dawned and set, and each acted out his own drama which the others might never know of or might only get a glimpse of or guess at.

For Talita, there was that little drama which almost blackened things for herself and her man and children. But because they loved each other so intensely, the ugliest bend was well negotiated, and the cloud passed on, the sun shone again. This was when a love letter fell into her hands owing to one of those clumsy things that often happen when lovers become stupid enough to write to each other. Talita wondered about something, as she sat huddled in the corner of her dining-sitting room and looked at the flame of a candle nearby, now quivering, now swaying this way and that and now coming into an erect position as if it lived a separate life from the stick of wax. She wondered how or why it happened that a mistress should entrust a confidential letter to a stupid messenger who in turn sends someone else without telling him to return the letter if the man should be out; why the second messenger should give the letter to her youngest child who then opens it and calls his mother from the bedroom to read it. Accident? Just downright brazen cheek on the part of the mistress . . . !

A hymn was struck and the wake began in earnest. There was singing, praying, singing, preaching in which the deceased was mentioned several times, often in vehement praise of him and his kindness. The room filled rapidly, until the air was one thick choking lump of grief. Once during the evening someone fainted. "An aunt of the deceased, the one who loved him most," a whisper escaped from someone who seemed to know and it was relayed from mouth to mouth right out into the yard where some people stood or sat. "Shame! Shame!" one could hear the comment from active sympathizers. More than once during the evening a woman screamed at high pitch. "The sister of the deceased," a whisper escaped, and it was relayed. "Shame! Shame!" was the murmured comment. "*Ao*, God's people!" an old man exclaimed. During the prayers inside the people outside continued to speak in low tones.

"Have the police caught the boys?"

"No — what, when has a black corpse been important?"

"But they have been asking questions in Corner B today."

"Hm."

"When's a black corpse been important?"

"Das' right, just ask him."

"It is Saturday today and if it was a white man lying there in the mortuary the newspapers would be screaming about a manhunt morning and evening since Thursday, the city would be upside down, God's truth."

"No, look here you men, these boys don't mean to kill nobody. Their empty stomachs and no work to do turns their head on evil things."

"*Ag*, you and your politics. Let one of them break into your house or ra — ."

The speaker broke off short and wiped his mouth with his hands as if to remove pieces of a foul word hanging carelessly from his lip.

"Das not the point," squeaked someone else.

Just then the notes of a moving hymn rolled out of the room and the men left the subject hanging and joined enthusiastically in the singing, taking different parts.

Some women were serving tea and sandwiches. A middle-aged man was sitting at a table in a corner of the room. He had a notebook in front of him, in which he entered the names of those who donated money and the amounts they gave. Such collections were meant to help meet funeral expenses. In fact they went into buying tea, coffee, bread and even groceries for meals served to guests who came from far.

"Who put him there?" asked an uncle of the deceased in an anxious tone, pointing at the money collector.

"Do I know?" an aunt said.

The question was relayed in whispers in different forms. Every one of the next-of-kin denied responsibility. It was soon discovered that the collector had mounted the stool on his own initiative.

"But don't you know that he has long fingers?" the same uncle flung the question in a general direction, just as if it were a loud thought.

"I'm going to tell him to stop taking money. *Hei*, cousin Stoffel, take that notebook at once, otherwise we shall never know what has happened to the money." Cousin Stoffel was not fast, but he had a reputation for honesty.

It was generally known that the deposed man appeared at every death house where he could easily be suspected to be related to the deceased, and invariably used his initiative to take collections and dispose of some of the revenue. But of course several of the folks who came to console Talita could be seen at other vigils and funerals by those who themselves were regular customers. The communal spirit? Largely. But also they were known to like their drinks very much. So a small fund was usually raised from the collections to buy liquor from a shebeen nearby and bring it to the wake.

Bang in the middle of a hymn a man came into the room and hissed while he made a beckoning sign to someone. Another hiss, yet another. An interested person who was meanly being left out immediately sensed conspiracy and followed those who answered the call. As they went out, they seemed to peel off a layer of the hymn and carry it out with them as they sang while moving out. In some corner of the yard or in the bedroom, a group of men, and sometimes a woman or two, conducted a familiar ritual.

"God's people," an uncle said solemnly, screwing up his face in an attempt to identify those who had been called. If he saw a stray one or two, he merely frowned but could do nothing about it on such a solemn occasion. The gate-crashers just stood, half-shy, and half-sure of themselves, now rubbing a nose, now changing postures.

"God's people, as I was about to say, here is an ox for slaughter." At this point he introduced a bottle of brandy. One did not simply plant a whole number of bottles on the floor: that was imprudent. "Cousin Felang came driving it to this house of sorrow. I have been given the honour of slaughtering it, as the uncle of this clan." With this he uncorked the bottle and served the brandy, taking care to measure with his fingers.

"This will kill the heart for a time so that it does not break from grief. Do not the English say *drown de sorry*?" He belched from deep down his stomach.

And then tongues began to wag. Anecdotes flew as freely as the drinks. And when they could not contain their mirth they laughed. "Yes, God's people," one observed, "the great death is often funny."

They did not continually take from the collections. If they felt they were still thirsty, someone went round among those he suspected felt the thirst too, and collected money from them to buy more drinks for another bout.

At midnight the people dispersed. The next-of-kin and close friends would alternate in sleeping in Talita's house.

They simply huddled against the wall in the same room and covered themselves with blankets.

Talita sat and waited at her corner like a fixture in the house. The children were staying with a relative and would come back on Sunday to see their father for the last time in his coffin. The corpse would be brought home on Saturday afternoon.

Thoughts continued to mill round in Talita's mind. A line of thought continued from where it had been cut off. One might imagine disjointed lines running around in circles. But always she wanted to keep the image of her man in front of her. Just as though it were an insult to the memory of him when the image escaped her even once.

Her man had confessed without making any scene at all. Perhaps it was due to the soft and timid manner in which Talita had asked him about the letter. She said she was sorry she had taken the letter from the child and, even when she had seen that instead of beginning "Dear Talita" it was "My everything", she had yielded to the temptation to read it. She was very sorry, she said, and added something to the effect that if she hadn't known, and he continued to carry on with the mistress, it wouldn't have been so bad. But the knowing it . . . Her man had promised not to see his mistress again. Not that his affair had detracted in any way from the relationship between man and wife, or made the man neglect the welfare of his family. Talita remembered how loyal he had been. The matter was regarded as closed and life had proceeded unhaltingly.

A few months later, however, she had noticed things, almost imperceptible; had heard stray words outside the house, almost inaudible or insignificant, which showed that her man was seeing his mistress. Talita had gone out of her way to track "the other woman" down. No one was going to share her man with her, fullstop, she said to herself.

She had found her: Marta, also a married woman. One evening Talita, when she was sure she could not be wrong in her suspicions, had followed Marta from the railway station to the latter's house in another part of Corner B. She entered shortly after the unsuspecting hostess. Marta's husband was in. Talita greeted both and sat down.

"I am glad you are in, *Morena* — sir. I have just come to ask you to chain your bitch. That is my man and mine alone." She stood up to leave.

"Wait, my sister," Marta's husband said. "Marta!" he called to his wife who had walked off saying laughingly and defiantly, "Aha, ooh," perhaps to suppress any feeling of embarrassment, as Talita thought. She wouldn't come out.

"You know, my sister," the man said with disturbing calm, "you know a bitch often answers to the sniffing of a male. And I think we both have to do some fastening." He gave Talita a piercing look which made her drop her eyes. She left the house. So he knows too, she thought. That look he gave her told her they shared the same apprehensions. Her man had never talked about the incident, although she was sure that Marta must have told him of it. Or would she have the courage to?

Often there were moments of deep silence as Talita and her man sat together or lay side by side. But he seldom stiffened up. He would take her into his arms and love her furiously and she would respond generously and tenderly, because she loved him and the pathos in his eyes.

"You know, my man," she ventured to say one evening in bed, "if there is anything I can help you with, if there is anything you would like to tell me, you mustn't be afraid to to tell me. There may be certain things a woman can do for her man which he never suspected she could do."

"Oh, don't worry about me. There is nothing you need do for me." And, like someone who had at last found a refuge after a rough and dangerous journey, her man would fold her in his arms and love her.

Was this it, she wondered? But how? Did it begin during her long period of ill health — this Marta thing? Or did it begin with a school episode? How could she tell? Her man never talked about his former boy-girl attachments, except in an oblique or vague way which yielded not a clue. Marta was pretty, no doubt. She was robust, had a firm waist and seemed to possess in physical appearance all that could attract a man. But if she, Talita, failed to give her man something Marta had to offer, she could not trace it. How could she? Her man was not the complaining type, and she often found out things that displeased him herself and set out to put them out of his way if she could. In the morning, while he was asleep, she would stare into his broad face to see if she could read something. But all she saw was the face she loved. Funny that you saw your man's face every day almost and yet you couldn't look at it while he slept without the sensation of some guilt or something timid or tense or something held in suspension: so that if the man stirred, your heart gave a leap as you turned your face away. One thing she was sure of amidst all the wild and agonizing speculation: her man loved her and their children . . .

"They're always doing this to me I do not matter I cannot allow plans to be made over the body of my cousin without my being told about it and why do they talk behind my back I don't stand for dusty nonsense me. And someone's daughter has the cheek to say I am nobody in the family of my cousin and say to me, I am always going ahead of others yes I am always running ahead of the others because I think other people are fools what right has she to talk behind my back why does she not tell me face to face what she thinks of me she is afraid I can make her see her mother if once I . . ."

"Sh!" The senior uncle of the dead man cut in to try to keep the peace. And he was firm. "What do you want to turn this house into? There is a widow in there in grief and here you are you haven't got what the English call respection. Do you want all the people around to laugh at us, think little of us? All of us bury our quarrels when we come together to weep over a dear one who has left; what nawsons is this?"

The cousin who felt outraged stood against the wall with her hands hidden behind her apron like a child caught in an act of mischief. She had not been addressing herself to anyone in particular and hoped someone would pick up the challenge. And although she felt rebuked, she said, "But uncle-of-the-clan, these people are always whispering dirty things behind my back what should I say? And then they go and order three buses instead of four these God's people have collected money for us to hire enough buses for them I shall not be surprised if someone helped himself to some of the money — "

"Sh!" the senior uncle interrupted. "We do not throw urine out of the chamber for everybody to see."

Someone whispered. *Mapodisa!* Police! With two boys! Everyone in the yard stood still, as if to some command. An

African constable came in, preceded by two dirty-looking youngsters in handcuffs.

"Stop!" he barked when they neared the door.

"Where is the widow?" the constable asked, addressing no one in particular.

Silence.

"*Hela!* Are these people dumb?" Silence. One of the boys blew his nose on to the ground with his free hand and wiped off the stuff from his upper lip and ran the hand down the flank of his trousers.

The constable went into the room with a firm stride, almost lifting the boys clear of the ground in the process. Inside, he came face to face with Talita, who was sitting in her usual corner. She seemed to look through him, and this unsettled him slightly. He braced himself up visibly.

"Face the mother there you fakabond!" he barked at the boys.

"I say look at the mother there, you dirty *tsotsi*." He angrily lifted the drooping head of one of them.

"You know this mother?" The boys shook their heads and mumbled.

"Mother, look at these *tsotsis*. Have you ever seen them before? Look at them carefully, take your time."

Talita looked at them wearily. She shook her head.

"Sure-sure?" Again she shook her head.

"I know what you do at night, you fakabond." The whole house was now full of him, the rustle of his khaki uniform and his voice and his official importance. "You kill, you steal, you rape and give other people no peace. Fakabond! You saw boys attack a man the other night, did you? Dung, let me tell you! You talk dung. Pure dung! You took out your knives for the man, fakabond! You see that bucket in front of your cells? You will fill it in quick time tonight when the *baas* is finished with you. This big white sergeant doesn't play around with black boys like you as I do. Dung! You didn't mean to kill him, you say, just wanted to beat him up and he fought back. Dung!"

The constable had hardly said the last word when an elderly woman came out of another room, holding a stick for support.

"What is all this?" she asked. "First you come and shake this poor child out of her peace when she has lost her man and then you use foul words at a time like this. Cannot this business wait until after the burial? Tell me who are you? Who is your father? Where were you born?"

He mumbled a few words, but the woman cut him short.

"Is this how you would like your mother or your wife to be treated, I mean your own own mother?"

"I am doing the government's work."

"Go and tell that government of yours that he is full of dung to send you to do such things. *Sies! Kgoboromente, kgoboromente!* You and him can go to hell where you belong. Get out!"

She took a lunge and landed her stick on him. Once, then twice, and the third time she missed because the constable dashed noisily out of the house, hauling the boys by the handcuffs. The woman pursued him with a limp, right up to the car in which was a white man in plain clothes — directly in front of the gate. The white man was obviously at pains to suppress a laugh. The constable entered with the boys in a most disorderly, undignified manner . . . The vehicle started off amidst the clatter of words that continued to come from the woman's mouth.

Talita wondered: were the boys merely the arms of some

monster sitting in the dark somewhere, wreaking vengeance on her man . . .?

Evening came. One caucus after another was held to make sure all arrangements were intact; for this was Saturday and the corpse had arrived. The double-decker buses from the city transport garages: were they booked? You son of Kobe did you get the death certificate and permit for the cemetery? And the number plate? They want to see the dead man's pass first. Ask for it in the house . . . Pass pass be damned, cannot a man go to his grave in peace without dragging his chains after him . . . ! Is the pastor coming tonight? Those three goats: have they been slaughtered? Right, this is how men work . . . You have worked well. The caucus meetings went on . . .

Word went round that the grandmother of the deceased had come. She loved Talita, so everyone who mattered testified. Heads nodded. Relatives who had not seen one another for a long time were there and family bonds were in place again. Some who were enemies tolerated each other, shooting side-glances at each other. Those who loved each other tended to exaggerate and exhibit the fact.

The people came in to keep vigil for the last night. The brown coffin — not ostentatious enough to cause a ripple of tell-tale excitement — stood against a wall. A white sheet was thrown across to partition the room so that in the smaller portion the corpse lay on a mattress under a white sheet. Talita sat next to it, leaning against her man's grandmother. The days and nights of waiting had told on her face; the black head-tie that was fastened like a hood cast a shade over it. Her hair had already been reduced to look like a schoolgirl's with a pair of scissors. Singing began. The elderly ladies washed the corpse. The tune sailed out of the room, floated in the air and was caught by those outside.

"Tomorrow after the funeral, eh? O.K.?"

"Yes, tomorrow after the funeral. Where?"

"At the party."

"Oh-*ja*. I forgot Cy's party. I'll go home first and change, eh? But I'm scared of my Pa."

"Let the old beard go fly a kite."

"He's my Pa all the same." She pushed him slightly as a reproach.

"O.K. He is, so let's not fight 'bout it. Still, don't you want me to come to your house?"

"You know he don't like you and he'd kill me if he saw me with you."

"Because you work and I don't, I'm sure. I'm getting a job Monday: that'll fix the old beard."

"No, it's not just a job and it's not you Pa hates."

"That's funny talk. What then?"

"Just because I'm twenty-three and I shouldn't have a boy yet."

"Jesus! Where's the old man been living all these years? Jesus!"

"Doesn't matter, Bee. You're my boy." She giggled.

"What's funny?"

"Just remembered my Pa asked me the other day who's that he saw me with. I say your name — Bee, I say."

"And then?"

"And then his face becomes sour and he says Who? I say Bee. He says Where have you heard someone called Bee — *Bee* did you say? I say anybody can call his son what he likes. He says you must be mad or a *tsotsi* without even a decent name."

A deep sigh and then: "That's not funny." He trembled slightly.

"Don't be cross Bee, you know it means nothing to me what you're called."

"Sh — they're praying now."

Two mouths and two tongues suck each other as he presses her against the wall of the shed that served as a fowl-run.

"Hm, they're praying," but her words are lost in the other's mouth. He feels her all over and she wriggles against him. She allows herself to be floored . . .

A hymn strikes again.

Two figures heave themselves up from the ground, panting. It has been a dark, delicious, fugitive time. They go back and join the singers, almost unnoticed.

The hymn continues. A hymn of hope, of release by death, of refuge for the weary and tormented: a surrender to death once it has been let loose among a flock of sheep. Underlying the poetry of this surrender is the one long and huge irony of endurance.

In another corner of the yard an elderly man was uncorking a bottle of whisky and pouring it into glasses. The sound of it, like water flowing down a rock crevice, was pleasing to the ear as the company squatted in front of the "priest". Here my children, kill the heart and as the Englishman says, *drown de sorry*. Ah, you see now . . . Someone, for lack of something important or relevant to say, but out of sheer blissful expectation, sighed: "*Ja Madoda* — yes, men, death is a strange thing. If he came to my house he would ask my woman to give him food any time and he could come any time of night and say I've come to see if you're all right and then we would talk and talk and talk. We were so close. And now he's late, just like that." And he sobbed and sniffled.

"*Ja,*" the others sighed in chorus.

A woman screamed in the room and broke into sobs. The others carried her out.

"Quiet child," a middle-aged woman coaxed. "Quiet, quiet, quiet." Talita held out. When Sunday dawned she said in her heart God let it pass this time. The final act came and passed . . .

They were all walking away from the grave towards the tarmac path leading to the exit. Suddenly a woman, seemingly from nowhere, went and flung herself on the soft, red, damp mound of the new grave. It was Marta. She screamed like one calling a person across a river in a flood, knowing the futility of it all. "Why did you leave me alone?" Marta yelled, her arms thrown over her head. Her legs kicked as she cried unashamedly, like a child whose toy has been wrenched out of his hand. Soon there was one long horizontal gasp as whispered words escaped the crowd, underlining the grotesqueness of the scene. Some stood stolidly, others amused, others outraged.

Two men went and dragged Marta away, while she still cried, "Come back, come back why did you leave me alone?"

Talita stopped short. She wanted badly to leap clear of the hands that supported her, but she was too weak. The urge strained every nerve, every muscle of her body. The women who supported her whispered to her to ignore the female's theatrics. "Let us go, child," they said. "She wants you to talk." They propelled Talita towards the black "family car".

A few days later, a letter arrived, addressed to Talita. She was walking about in the yard, but was not allowed to go to work or anywhere beyond the gate. The letter was in a bad but legible scrawl and read:

"Dear Missis Molamo, I am dropping this few lines for to hoping that you are living good now i want to telling you my hart is sore sore. i hold myselfe bad on the day of youre mans funeral my hart was ful of pane too much and i see myselfe already o Missis Molamo alreaddy doing mad doings i think the gods are beatting me now for holding myselfe as wyle animall forgeef forgeef i pray with all my hart child of the people."

Talita paused. These wild women who can't even write must needs try to do so in English. She felt the tide of anger and hatred mounting up, flushing her whole body, and then she wondered if she should continue to read. She planted her elbow on the table and supported her head with her hand. She felt drawn to the letter, so she obeyed the impulse to continue.

"now i must tel you something you must noe quik quik thees that i can see that when you come to my hause and then whenn you see me kriing neer the grafe i can see you think i am sweet chokolet of your man i can see you think in your hart my man love that wooman no no i want to tel you that he neva love me nevaneva he livd same haus my femily rented in Fitas and i lovd him mad i tel you i lovd him mad i wanted him with red eyes he was nise leetl bit nise to me but i see he sham for me as i have got no big ejucashin he

got too much book i make nise tea and cake fo him
and he like my muther and he is so nise i want to foss
him to love me but he just nise i am shoor he come to
meet me in toun now we are 2 marryd peeople bicos
he remember me and muther looked aftar him like
bruther for me he was stil nise to me but al wooman
can see whenn there is no loveness in a man and they
can see lovfulness. now he is gonn i feel i want to rite
with my al ten fingas becos i have too muche to say
aboute your sorriness and my sorriness i will help you
to kry you help me to kry and leev that man in peas
with his gods. so i stop press here my deer i beg to pen
off the gods look after us

> i remain your sinserity
> Missis Marta Shuping.'

When Talita finished reading, a great dawn was breaking
upon her, and she stood up and made tea for herself. She
felt like a foot traveller after a good refreshing bath.

Mrs Plum

My madam's name was Mrs Plum. She loved dogs and Africans and said that everyone must follow the law even if it hurt. These were three big things in Madam's life.

I came to work for Mrs Plum in Greenside, not very far from the centre of Johannesburg, after leaving two white families. The first white people I worked for as a cook and laundry woman were a man and his wife in Parktown North. They drank too much and always forgot to pay me. After five months I said to myself, No. I am going to leave these drunks. So that was it. That day I was angry as a red-hot iron when it meets water. The second house I cooked and washed for had five children who were badly brought up. This was in Belgravia. Many times they called me You Black Girl and I kept quiet. Because their mother heard them and said nothing. Also I was only new from Phokeng my home, very far away near Rustenburg. I wanted to learn and know the white people before I knew how far to go with the others I would work for afterwards. The thing that drove me mad and made me pack and go was a man who came to visit them often. They said he was a cousin or something like that. He came to the kitchen many times and tried to make me laugh. He patted me on the buttocks. I told the master. The man did it again and I asked the madam that very day to give me my money and let me go.

These were the first nine months after I had left Phokeng to work in Johannesburg. There were many of us girls and young women from Phokeng, from Zeerust, from Shuping, from Kosten, and many other places who came to work in the cities. So the suburbs were full of blackness. Most of us had already passed Standard Six and so we learned more English where we worked. None of us liked to work for white farmers, because we knew too much about them on the farms near our homes. They do not pay well and they are cruel people.

At Easter time so many of us went home for a long weekend to see our people and to eat chicken and sour milk and *morogo* — wild spinach. We also took home sugar and condensed milk and tea and coffee and sweets and custard powder and tinned foods.

It was a home-girl of mine, Chimane, who called me to take a job in Mrs Plum's house, just next door to where she worked. This is the third year now. I have been quite happy with Mrs Plum and her daughter Kate. By this I mean that my place as a servant in Greenside is not as bad as that of many others. Chimane too does not complain much. We are paid six pounds a month with free food and free servant's room. No one can ever say that they are well paid, so we go on complaining somehow. Whenever we meet on Thursday afternoons, which is time-off for all of us black women in the suburbs, we talk and talk and talk: about our people at home and their letters; about their illnesses; about bad crops; about a sister who wanted a school uniform and books and school fees; about some of our madams and masters who are good, or stingy with money or food, or stupid or full of nonsense, or who kill themselves and each other, or who are dirty — and so many things I cannot count them all.

Thursday afternoon we go to town to look at the shops, to attend a women's club, to see our boy friends, to go to bioscope some of us. We turn up smart, to show others the clothes we bought from the black men who sell soft goods to servants in the suburbs. We take a number of things and they come round every month for a bit of money until we finish paying. Then we dress the way of many white madams and girls. I think we look really smart. Sometimes we catch the eyes of a white woman looking at us and we laugh and laugh and laugh until we nearly drop onto the ground because we feel good inside ourselves.

What did the girl next door call you, Mrs Plum asked me the first day I came to her. Jane, I replied. Was there not an African name? I said yes, Karabo. All right, Madam said. We'll call you Karabo, she said. She spoke as if she knew a name is a big thing. I knew so many whites who did not care what they called black people as long as it was all right for their tongue. This pleased me, I mean Mrs Plum's use of Karabo; because the only time I heard the name was when I was at home or when my friends spoke to me. Then she showed me what to do: meals, meal times, washing, and where all the things were that I was going to use.

My daughter will be here in the evening, Madam said. She is at school. When the daughter came, she added, she would tell me some of the things she wanted me to do for her every day.

Chimane, my friend next door, had told me about the daughter Kate, how wild she seemed to be, and about Mr

Plum who had killed himself with a gun in a house down the street. They had left the house and come to this one.

Madam is a tall woman. Not slender, not fat. She moves slowly, and speaks slowly. Her face looks very wise, her forehead seems to tell me she has a strong liver: she is not afraid of anything. Her eyes are always swollen at the lower eyelids like a white person who has not slept for many many nights or like a large frog. Perhaps it is because she smokes too much, like wet wood that will not know whether to go up in flames or stop burning. She looks me straight in the eyes when she talks to me, and I know she does this with other people too. At first this made me fear her, now I am used to her. She is not a lazy woman, and she does many things outside, in the city and in the suburbs.

This was the first thing her daughter Kate told me when she came and we met. Don't mind mother, Kate told me, she is sometimes mad with people for very small things. She will soon be all right and speak nicely to you again.

Kate, I like her very much, and she likes me too. She tells me many things a white woman does not tell a black servant. I mean things about what she likes and does not like, what her mother does or does not do, all these. At first I was unhappy and wanted to stop her, but now I do not mind.

Kate looks very much like her mother in the face. I think her shoulders will be just as round and strong-looking. She moves faster than Madam. I asked her why she was still at school when she was so big. She laughed. Then she tried to tell me that the school where she went was for big people, who had finished with lower school. She was learning big things about cooking and food. She can explain better, me I cannot. She came home on weekends.

Since I came to work for Mrs Plum Kate has been teaching me plenty of cooking. I first learned from her and Madam the word *recipes.* When Kate was at the big school, Madam taught me how to read cookery books. I went on very slowly at first, slower than an ox-wagon. Now I know more. When Kate came home, she found I had read the recipe she left me. So we just cooked straightaway. Kate thinks I am fit to cook in a hotel. Madam thinks so too. Never, never, I thought. Cooking in a hotel is like feeding oxen. No one can say thank you to you. After a few months I could cook the Sunday lunch and later I could cook specials for Madam's or Kate's guests.

Madam did not only teach me cooking. She taught me how to look after guests. She praised me when I did very well, not like the white people I had worked for before. I do not know what runs crooked in the heads of other people. Madam also had classes in the evenings for servants to teach them how to read and write. She and two other women in Greenside taught in a church hall.

As I say, Kate tells me plenty of things about Madam. She says to me she says, My mother goes to meetings many times. I ask her I say, What for? She says to me she says, For your people. I ask her I say, My people are in Phokeng far away. They have got mouths, I say. Why does she want to say something for them? Does she know what my mother and what my father want to say? They can speak when they want to. Kate raises her shoulders and drops them and says, How can I tell you, Karabo? I don't say your people — your family only. I mean all the black people in this country. I say Oh! What do the black people want to say? Again she raises her shoulders and drops them, taking a deep breath.

I ask her I say, With whom is she in the meetings?

She says, With other people who think like her.

I ask her I say, Do you say there are people in the world who think the same things?

She nods her head.

I ask, What things?

So that a few of your people should one day be among those who rule this country, get more money for what they do for the white man and — what did Kate say again? Yes, that Madam and those who think like her also wanted my people who have been to school to choose those who must speak for them in the — I think she said it looks like a *kgotla* at home who rule the villages.

I say to Kate I say, Oh I see now. I say, Tell me Kate why is Madam always writing on the machine, all the time everyday nearly?

She replies she says, Oh my mother is writing books.

I ask, you mean a book like those? — pointing at the books on the shelves.

Yes, Kate says.

And she told me how Madam wrote books and other things for newspapers and she wrote for the newspapers and magazines to say things for the black people who should be treated well, be paid more money, for the black people who can read and write many things to choose those who want to speak for them.

Kate also told me she said, My mother and other women who think like her put on black belts over their shoulders when they are sad and they want to show the white government they do not like the things being done by whites to blacks. My mother and the others go and stand where the people in government are going to enter or go out of the building.

I ask her I say, Does the government and the white people listen and stop their sins? She says No. But my mother is in another group of white people.

I ask, Do the people of the government give the women tea and cakes? Kate says, Karabo, how stupid! Oh!

I say to her I say, Among my people if someone comes and stands in front of my house I tell him to come in and I give him food. You white people are wonderful. But they keep standing there and the government people do not give them anything.

She replies, You mean strange. How many times have I taught you not to say *wonderful* when you mean *strange* ! Well, Kate says with a short heart and looking cross and she shouts, Well they do not stand there the whole day to ask for tea and cakes, stupid. Oh dear!

Always when Madam finished to read her newspapers she gave them to me to read to help me speak and write better English. When I had read she asked me to tell her some of the things in it. In this way, I did better and better and my mind was opening and opening and I was learning and learning many things about the black people inside and outside the towns which I did not know in the least. When I found words that were too difficult or I did not understand some of the things I asked Madam. She always told me, You see this, you see that, eh? with a heart that can carry on a long way. Yes, Madam writes many letters to the papers. She is always sore about the way the white police beat up black people; about the way black people who work for whites are made to sit at the Zoo Lake with their hearts hanging, because the white people say our people are making noise on Sunday afternoon when they want to rest in their houses and gardens; about many ugly things that happen when some white people meet black man on the pavement or street. So Madam writes to the papers to let others know, to ask the government to be kind to us.

In the first year Mrs Plum wanted me to eat at table with her. It was very hard, one because I was not used to eating at table with a fork and knife, two because I heard of no other kitchen worker who was handled like this. I was afraid. Afraid of everybody, of Madam's guests if they found me doing this. Madam said I must not be silly. I must show that African servants can also eat at table. Number three, I could not eat some of the things I loved very much: mealie-meal porridge with sour milk or *morogo*, stamped mealies mixed with butter beans, sour porridge for breakfast and other things. Also, except for morning porridge, our food is nice when you eat with the hand. So nice that it does not stop in the mouth or the throat to greet anyone before it passes smoothly down.

We often had lunch together with Chimane next door and our garden boy — Ha! I must remember never to say *boy* again when I talk about a man. This makes me think of a day during the first few weeks in Mrs Plum's house. I was talking about Dick her garden man and I said "garden boy". And she says to me she says, Stop talking about a "boy", Karabo. Now listen here, she says, you Africans must learn to speak properly about each other. And she says White people won't talk kindly about you if you look down upon each other.

I say to her I say, Madam, I learned the word from the white people I worked for, and all the kitchen maids say "boy".

She replies, she says to me, Those are white people who know nothing, just low-class whites. I say to her I say, I thought white people know everything.

She said, You'll learn my girl and you must start in this house, hear? She left me thinking, my mind mixed up.

I learned. I grew up.

If any woman or girl does not know the Black Crow Club in Bree Street, she does not know anything. I think nearly everything takes place inside and outside that house. It is just where the dirty part of the city begins, with factories and the market. After the market is the place where Indians and "coloured" people live. It is also at the Black Crow that the buses turn round and go back to the black townships. Noise, noise, noise all the time. There are women who sell hot sweet potatoes and fruit and monkey nuts and boiled eggs in the winter, boiled mealies and the other things in the summer, all these on the pavements. The streets are always full of potato and fruit skins and monkey nut shells. There is always a strong smell of roast pork. I think it is because of Piel's cold storage down Bree Street.

Madam said she knew the black people who work in the Black Crow. She was happy that I was spending my afternoon on Thursdays in such a club. You will learn sewing, knitting, she said, and other things that you like. Do you like to dance? I told her I said, Yes, I want to learn. She paid the two shillings fee for me each month.

We waited on the first floor, we were the ones who were learning sewing; waiting for the teacher. We talked and laughed about madams and masters, and their children and their dogs and birds and whispered about our boy friends.

Sies! My madam you do not know — *mojuta oa'nete* — a real miser . . .

Jo — jo — jo! you should see our new dog. A big thing like this. People! Big in a foolish way . . .

What! Me, I take a master's bitch by the leg, me, and throw it away so that it keeps howling, *tjwe — tjwe! ngo — wu ngo — wy!* I don't play about with them, me . . .

Shame, poor thing! God sees you, true . . .!

They wanted me to take their dog out for a walk every afternoon and I told them I said, It is not my work in other houses the garden man does it. I just said to myself I said, they can go to the chickens. Let them bite their elbow before I take out a dog. I am not so mad yet . . .

Hei! It is not like the child of my white people who keeps a big white rat and you know what? He puts it on his bed when he goes to school. And let the blankets just begin to smell of urine and all the nonsense and they tell me to wash them. *Hei*, people!

Did you hear about Rebone, people! Her madam put her out because her master was always tapping her buttocks with his fingers. And yesterday the madam saw the master press Rebone against himself . . .

Jo — jo — jo! people . . . !

Dirty white man!

No, not dirty. The madam smells too old for him.

Hei! Go and wash your mouth with soap, this girl's mouth is dirty . . .

Jo, Rebone, daughter of the people! We must help her to find a job before she thinks of going back home.

The teacher came. A woman with strong legs, a strong face, and kind eyes. She had short hair and dressed in a simple but lovely floral frock. She stood well on her legs and hips. She had a black mark between the two top front teeth. She smiled as if we were her children. Our group began with games, and then Lilian Ngoyi took us for sewing. After this she gave a brief talk to all of us from the different classes.

I can never forget the things this woman said and how she put them to us. She told us that the time had passed for black girls and women in the suburbs to be satisfied with working, sending money to our people and going to see them once a year. We were to learn, she said, that the world would never be safe for black people until they were in the government with the power to make laws. The power should be given to the Africans who were more than whites.

We asked her questions and she answered them with wisdom. I shall put some of them down in my own words as I remember them.

Shall we take the place of the white people in the government?

Some yes. But we shall be more than they as we are more in the country. But also the people of all colours will come together and there are good white men we can choose and there are Africans some white people will choose to be in the government.

There are good madams and masters and bad ones. Should we take the good ones for friends?

A master and a servant can never be friends. Never, so put that out of your head, will you. You are not even sure if the ones you say are good are not like that because they cannot breathe or live without the work of your hands. As long as you need their money, face them with respect. But you must know that many sad things are happening in our country and you, all of you, must always be learning, adding what you already know, and obey us when we ask you to help us.

At other times Lilian Ngoyi told us she said, Remember your poor people at home and the way in which the whites are moving them from place to place like sheep and cattle. And at other times again she told us she said, Remember that a hand cannot wash itself, it needs another to do it.

I always thought of Madam when Lilian Ngoyi spoke. I asked myself, What would she say if she knew that I was listening to such words. Words like: A white man is looked after by his black nanny and his mother when he is a baby. When he grows up the white government looks after him, sends him to school, makes it impossible for him to suffer from the great hunger, keeps a job ready and open for him as soon as he wants to leave school. Now Lilian Ngoyi asked she said, How many white people can be born in a white hospital, grow up in white streets, be clothed in lovely cotton, lie on white cushions; how many whites can live all their lives in a fenced place away from people of other colours and then, as men and women learn quickly the correct ways of thinking, learn quickly to ask questions in their minds, big questions that will throw over all the nice things of a white man's life? How many? Very very few! For those who have begun and are joining us with both feet in our house, we can only say, Welcome!

I was learning. I was growing up. Every time I thought of Madam, she became more and more like a dark forest which one fears to enter, and which one will never know. But there were several times when I thought, This woman is easy to understand, she is like all the other white women.

What else are they teaching you at the Black Crow, Karabo?

I tell her I say, nothing, Madam. I ask her I say, Why does Madam ask?

You are changing.

What does Madam mean?

Well, you are changing.

But we are always changing, Madam.

And she left me standing in the kitchen. This was a few days after I had told her that I did not want to read more than one white paper a day. The only magazines I wanted to read, I said to her, were those from overseas, if she had them. I told her that white papers had pictures of white people most of the time. They talked mostly about white people and their gardens, dogs, weddings and parties. I asked her if she could buy me a Sunday paper that spoke about my people. Madam bought it for me. I did not think that she would do it.

There were mornings when, after hanging the white people's washing on the line, Chimane and I stole a little time to stand at the fence and talk. We always stood where we could be hidden by our rooms.

Hei, Karabo, you know what? That was Chimane.

No — what? Before you start, tell me, has Timi come back to you?

Ag, I do not care. He is still angry. But boys are fools, they always come back dragging themselves on their empty bellies. *Hei*, you know what?

Yes?

The Thursday past I saw Moruti K.K. I laughed until I dropped on the ground. He is standing in front of the Black Crow. I believe his big stomach was crying from hunger. Now he has a small dog in his armpit, and is standing before a woman selling boiled eggs and — *hei* home-girl! —

tripe and intestines are boiling in a pot — oh, — the smell, you could fill a hungry belly with it, the way it was good. I think Moruti K.K. is waiting for the woman to buy a boiled egg. I do not know what the woman was still doing. I am standing nearby. The dog keeps wriggling and pushing out its nose, looking at the boiling tripe. Moruti keeps patting it with his free hand, not so? Again the dog wants to spill out of Moruti's hand and it gives a few sounds through the nose. *Hei* man, home-girl! One two three the dog spills out to catch some of the good meat! It misses falling into the hot gravy in which the tripe is swimming I do not know how. Moruti K.K. tries to chase it. It has tumbled on the woman's eggs and potatoes and all are in the dust. She stands up and goes after K.K. She is shouting to him to pay, not so? Where am I at that time? I am nearly dead with laughter the tears are coming down so far.

I was myself holding tight on the fence so as not to fall through laughing. I held my stomach to keep back a pain in the side.

I ask her I say, Did Moruti K.K. come back to pay for the wasted food?

Yes, he paid.

The dog?

He caught it. That is a good African dog. A dog must look for its own food when it is not time for meals. Not these stupid spoiled angels the whites keep giving tea and biscuits.

Hmm.

Dick our garden man joined us, as he often did. When the story was repeated to him the man nearly rolled on the ground laughing.

He asks who is Reverend K.K.?

I say he is the owner of the Black Crow.

Oh!

We reminded each other, Chimane and I, of the round minister. He would come into the club, look at us with a smooth smile on his smooth round face. He would look at each one of us, with that smile on all the time, as if he had forgotten that it was there. Perhaps he had, because as he looked at us, almost stripping us naked with his watery shining eyes — funny — he could have been a farmer looking at his ripe corn, thinking many things.

K.K. often spoke without shame about what he called ripe girls — *matjitjana* — with good firm breasts. He said such girls were pure without any nonsense in their heads and bodies. Everybody talked a great deal about him and what they thought he must be doing in his office whenever he called in so-and-so.

The Reverend K.K. did not belong to any church. He baptized, married, and buried, for a fee, people who had no church to do such things for them. They said he had been driven out of the Presbyterian Church. He had formed his own, but it did not go far. Later he came and opened the Black Crow. He knew just how far to go with Lilian Ngoyi. She said although she used his club to teach us things that would help us in life, she could not go on if he was doing any wicked things with the girls in his office. Moruti K.K. feared her, and kept his place.

When I began to tell my story, I thought I was going to tell you mostly about Mrs Plum's two dogs. But I have been talking about people. I think Dick is right when he says, What is a dog! And there are so many dogs, cats and parrots in Greenside and other places that Mrs Plum's dogs do not look special. But there was something special in the dog business in Madam's house. The way in which she loved them, maybe.

Monty is a tiny animal with long hair and small black eyes and a face nearly like that of an old woman. The other, Malan, is a bit bigger, with brown and white colours. It has small hair and looks naked by the side of his friend. They sleep in two separate baskets which stay in Madam's bedroom. They are to be washed often and brushed and sprayed and they sleep on pink linen. Monty has a pink ribbon which stays on his neck most of the time. They both carry a cover on their backs. They make me fed up when I see them in their baskets, looking fat, and as if they knew all that was going on everywhere.

It was Dick's work to look after Monty and Malan, to feed them, and to do everything for them. He did this together with garden work and cleaning of the house. He came at the beginning of this year. He just came, as if from nowhere, and Madam gave him the job as she had chased away two before him, she told me. In both those cases, she said that they could not look after Monty and Malan.

Dick had a long heart, even although he told me and Chimane that European dogs were stupid, spoiled. He said, one day those white people will put earrings and toe rings and bangles on their dogs. That would be the day he would leave Mrs Plum. For, he said, he was sure that she would want him to polish the rings and bangles with Brasso.

Although he had a long heart, Madam was still not sure of him. She often went to the dogs after a meal or after a cleaning and said to them, Did Dick give you food, sweethearts? Or, Did Dick wash you, sweethearts? Let me see. And I could see that Dick was blowing up like a balloon with anger. These things called white people! he said to me. Talking to dogs!

I say to him I say, People talk to oxen at home do I not say so?

Yes, he says, but at home do you not know that a man speaks to an ox because he wants to make it pull the plough or the wagon or to stop or to stand still for a person to inspan it? No one simply goes to an ox looking at him with eyes far apart and speaks to it. Let me ask you, do you ever see a person where we come from take a cow and press it to his stomach or his cheek? Tell me!

And I say to Dick I say, We were talking about an ox, not a cow.

He laughed with his broad mouth until tears came out of his eyes. At a certain point I laughed aloud too.

One day when you have time, Dick says to me, he says, you should look into Madam's bedroom when she has put a notice outside her door.

Dick, what are you saying, I ask.

I do not talk, me. I know deep inside me.

Dick was about our age, I and Chimane. So we always said *moshiman'o* when we spoke about his tricks. Because he was not too big to be a boy to us. He also said to us, *Hei, lona banyana kelona* – Hey, you girls, you! His large mouth always seemed to be making ready to laugh. I think Madam did not like this. Many times she would say, What is there to make you laugh here? Or in the garden she would say, This is a flower and when it wants water that is not funny! Or again, If you did more work and stopped trying to water my plants with your smile you would be more useful. Even when Dick did not mean to smile. What Madam did not get tired of saying was, If I left you to look after my dogs without anyone to look after you at the same time you would drown the poor things.

Dick smiled at Mrs Plum. Dick hurt Mrs Plum's dogs? Then cows can fly. He was really afraid of white people, Dick. I think he tried very hard not to feel afraid. For he was always showing me and Chimane in private how Mrs Plum walked, and spoke. He took two bowls and pressed them to his chest, speaking softly to them as Madam speaks to Monty and Malan. Or he sat at Madam's table and acted the way she sits when writing. Now and again he looked back over his shoulder, pulled his face long like a horse's making as if he were looking over his glasses while telling me something to do. Then he would sit on one of the arm-chairs, cross his legs and act the way Madam drank her tea; he held the cup he was thinking about between his thumb and pointing finger, only letting their nails meet. And he laughed after every act. He did these things, of course, when Madam was not home. And where was I at such times? Almost flat on my stomach, laughing.

But oh how Dick trembled when Mrs Plum scolded him! He did his house cleaning very well. Whatever mistake he made, it was mostly with the dogs; their linen, their food. One white man came into the house one afternoon to tell Madam that Dick had been very careless when taking the dogs for a walk. His own dog was waiting on Madam's stoep. He repeated that he had been driving down our street and Dick had let loose Monty and Malan to cross the street. The white man made plenty of noise about this and I think wanted to let Madam know how useful he had been. He kept on saying, Just one inch, *just* one inch. It was lucky I put on my brakes quick enough . . . But your boy kept on smiling — Why? Strange. My boy would only do it twice and

then . . . ! His pass. The man moved his hand like one
writing, to mean that he would sign his servant's pass for
him to go and never come back. When he left, the white
man said, Come on Rusty, the boy is waiting to clean you.
Dogs with names, men without, I thought.

Madam climbed on top of Dick for this, as we say.

Once one of the dogs, I don't know which — Malan or
Monty — took my stocking — brand new, you hear — and
tore it with its teeth and paws. When I told Madam about it,
my anger as high as my throat, she gave me money to buy
another pair. It happened again. This time she said she was
not going to give me money because I must also keep my
stockings where the two gentlemen would not reach them.
Mrs Plum did not want us ever to say *Voetsek* when we
wanted the dogs to go away. Me I said this when they came
sniffing at my legs or fingers. I hate it.

In my third year in Mrs Plum's house, many things
happened, most of them all bad for her. There was trouble
with Kate; Chimane had big trouble; my heart was twisted
by two loves; and Monty and Malan became real dogs for a
few days.

Madam had a number of suppers and parties. She invited
Africans to some of them. Kate told me the reasons for
some of the parties. Like her mother's books were finished,
a visitor from across the seas and so on. I did not like the
black people who came here to drink and eat. They spoke
such difficult English like people who were full of all the
books in the world. They looked at me as if I were right
down there whom they thought little of — me a black
person like them.

One day I heard Kate speak to her mother. She says I
don't know why you ask so many Africans to the house.

A few will do at a time. She said something about the government which I could not hear well. Madam replies she says to her, You know some of them do not meet white people often, so far away in their dark houses. And she says to Kate that they do not come because they want her as a friend but they just want a drink for nothing.

I simply felt that I could not be the servant of white people and of blacks at the same time. At my home or in my room I could serve them without a feeling of shame. And now, if they were only coming to drink!

But one of the black men and his sister always came to the kitchen to talk to me. I must have looked unfriendly the first time, for Kate talked to me about it afterwards as she was in the kitchen when they came. I know that at that time I was not easy at all. I was ashamed and I felt that a white person's house was not the place for me to look happy in front of other black people while the white man looked on.

Another time it was easier. The man was alone. I shall never forget that night, as long as I live. He spoke kind words and I felt my heart grow big inside me. It caused me to tremble. There were several other visits. I knew that I loved him, I could never know what he really thought of me, I mean as a woman and he as a man. But I loved him, and I still think of him with a sore heart. Slowly I came to know the pain of it. Because he was a doctor and so full of knowledge and English I could not reach him. So I knew he could not stoop down to see me as someone who wanted him to love me.

Kate turned very wild. Mrs Plum was very much worried. Suddenly it looked as if she were a new person, with new ways and new everything. I do not know what was wrong or right. She began to play the big gramophone aloud, as if the music were for the whole of Greenside. The music was wild and she twisted her waist all the time, with her mouth half open. She did the same things in her room. She left the big school and every Saturday night now she went out. When I looked at her face, there was something deep and wild there on it, and when I thought she looked young she looked old, and when I thought she looked old she was young. We were both twenty-two years of age. I think that I could see the reason why her mother was so worried, why she was suffering.

Worse was to come.

They were now openly screaming at each other. They began in the sitting room and went upstairs together, speaking fast hot biting words, some of which I did not grasp. One day Madam comes to me and says, You know Kate loves an African, you know the doctor who comes to supper here often. She says he loves her too and they will leave the country and marry outside. Tell me, Karabo, what do your people think of this kind of thing between a white woman and a black man? It *cannot* be right, can it?

I reply and I say to her, We have never seen it happen before where I come from.

That's right, Karabo, it is just madness.

Madam left. She looked like a hunted person.

These white women, I say to myself I say, these white women, why do not they love their own men and leave us to love ours!

From that minute I knew that I would never want to speak to Kate. She appeared to me as a thief, as a fox that falls upon a flock of sheep at night. I hated her. To make it worse, he would never be allowed to come to the house again.

Whenever she was home there was silence between us. I no longer wanted to know anything about what she was doing, where or how.

I lay awake for hours on my bed. Lying like that, I seemed to feel parts of my body beat and throb inside me, the way I have seen big machines doing, pounding and pounding and pushing and pulling and pouring some water into one hole which came out at another end. I stretched myself so many times so as to feel tired and sleepy.

When I did sleep, my dreams were full of painful things.

One evening I made up my mind, after putting it off many times. I told my boy-friend that I did not want him any longer. He looked hurt and that hurt me too. He left.

The thought of the African doctor was still with me and it pained me to know that I should never see him again, unless I met him in the street on a Thursday afternoon. But he had a car. Even if I did meet him by luck, how could I make him see that I loved him? *Ag*, I do not believe he would even stop to think what kind of woman I am. Part of that winter was a time of longing and burning for me. I say part because there are always things to keep servants busy whose white people go to the sea for the winter.

To tell the truth, winter was the time for servants; not nannies, because they went with their madams so as to look after the children. Those like me stayed behind to look after the house and dogs. In winter so many families went away that the dogs remained the masters and madams. You could see them walk like white people in the streets. Silent but with plenty of power. And when you saw them you knew that they were full of more nonsense and fancies in the house.

There was so little work to do.

One week word was whispered round that a home-boy of ours was going to hold a party in his room on Saturday. I think we all took it for a joke. How could the man be so bold and stupid? The police were always driving about at night looking for black people; and if the whites next door heard the party noise — *oho!* But still, we were full of joy and wanted to go. As for Dick, he opened his big mouth and nearly fainted when he heard of it and that I was really going.

During the day on the big Saturday Kate came.

She seemed a little less wild. But I was not ready to talk to her. I was surprised to hear myself answer her when she said to me, Mother says you do not like a marriage between a white girl and a black man, Karabo.

Then she was silent.

She says, but I want to help him, Karabo.

I ask her I say, You want to help him to do what?

To go higher and higher, to the top.

I knew I wanted to say so much that was boiling in my chest. I could not say it. I thought of Lilian Ngoyi at the Black Crow, what she said to us. But I was mixed up in my head and in my blood.

You still agree with my mother?

All I could say was, I said to your mother I had never seen a black man and a white man marrying, you hear me? What I think about it is my business.

I remembered that I wanted to iron my party dress and so I left her. My mind was full of the party again and I was glad because Kate and the doctor would not worry my peace that day. And the next day the sun would shine for all of us. Kate or no Kate, doctor or no doctor.

The house where our home-boy worked was hidden

from the main road by a number of trees. But although we asked a number of questions and counted many fingers of bad luck until we had no more hands for fingers, we put on our best pay-while-you-wear dresses and suits and clothes bought from boys who had stolen them, and went to our home-boy's party. We whispered all the way while we climbed up to the house. Someone who knew told us that the white people next door were away for the winter. Oh, so that is the thing, we said.

We poured into the garden through the back and stood in front of his rooms laughing quietly. He came from the big house behind us, and were we not struck dumb when he told us to go into the white people's house! Was he mad? We walked in with slow footsteps that seemed to be sniffing at the floor, not sure of anything. Soon we were standing and sitting all over on the nice warm cushions and the heaters were on. Our home-boy turned the lights low. I counted fifteen people inside. We saw how we loved one another's evening dress. The boys were smart too.

Our home-boy's girl-friend Naomi was busy in the kitchen preparing food. He took out glasses and cold drinks — fruit juices, tomato juice, ginger beers, and so many other kinds of soft drink. It was just too nice. The tarts, the biscuits, the snacks, the cakes, *woo*, that was a party, I tell you. I think I ate more ginger cake than I had ever done in my life. Naomi had baked some of the things. Our home-boy came to me and said I do not want the police to come here and have reason to arrest us, so I am not serving hot drinks, not even beer. There is no law that we cannot have parties, is there? So we can feel free. Our use of this house is the master's business. If I had asked him he would have thought me mad.

I say to him I say, You have a strong liver to do such a thing.

He laughed.

He played pennywhistle music on gramophone records — Miriam Makeba, Dorothy Masuka and other African singers and players. We danced and the party became more and more noisy and more happy. *Hai*, those girls Miriam and Dorothy, they can sing, I tell you! We ate more and more and told more stories. In the middle of the party, our home-boy called us to listen to what he was going to say. Then he told us how he and a friend of his in Orlando collected money to bet on a horse for the July Handicap in Durban. They did this each year but lost. Now they had won two hundred pounds. We all clapped hands and cheered. Two hundred pounds, *woo!*

You should go and sit at home and just eat time, I say to him. He laughs and says, You have no understanding, not one little bit.

To all of us he says, Now my brothers and sisters enjoy yourselves. At home I should slaughter a goat for us to feast and thank our ancestors. But this is town life and we must thank them with tea and cake and all those sweet things. I know some people think I must be so bold that I could be midwife to a lion that is giving birth, but enjoy yourselves and have no fear.

Madam came back looking strong and fresh.

The very week she arrived the police had begun again to search servants' rooms. They were looking for what they called loafers and men without passes who they said were living with friends in the suburbs against the law. Our dog's meat boys became scarce because of the police. A boy who had a girl-friend in the kitchens, as we say, always told his friends that he was coming for dog's meat when he meant he was visiting his girl. This was because we gave our boy-friends part of the meat the white people bought for the dogs and us.

One night two policemen, one white and one black, entered Mrs Plum's yard. They said they had come to search. She says, No, they cannot. They say, Yes, they must do it. She answers, No. They forced their way to the back, to Dick's room and mine. Mrs Plum took the hose that was running in the front garden and quickly went round to the back. I cut across the floor to see what she was going to say to the men. They were talking to Dick, using dirty words. Mrs Plum did not wait, she just pointed the hose at the two policemen. This seemed to surprise them. They turned round and she pointed it into their faces. Without their seeing me I went to the tap at the corner of the house and opened it more. I could see Dick, like me, was trying to keep down his laughter. They shouted and tried to wave the water away, but she kept the hose pointing at them, now moving it up and down. They turned and ran through the back gate, swearing the while.

That fixes them, Mrs Plum said.

The next day the morning newspaper reported it.

They arrived in the afternoon — the two policemen — with another. They pointed out Mrs Plum and she was led to the police station. They took her away to answer for stopping the police while they were doing their work.

She came back and said she had paid bail.

At the magistrate's court, Madam was told that she had done a bad thing. She would have to pay a fine or else go to prison for fourteen days. She said she would go to jail to show that she felt she was not in the wrong.

Kate came and tried to tell her that she was doing something silly going to jail for a small thing like that. She tells Madam she says, This is not even a thing to take to the high court. Pay the money. What is £5?

Madam went to jail.

She looked very sad when she came out. I thought of what Lilian Ngoyi often said to us: You must be ready to go to jail for the things you believe are true and for which you are taken by the police. What did Mrs Plum really believe about me, Chimane, Dick and all the other black people, I asked myself? I did not know. But from all those things she was writing for the papers and all those meetings she was going to where white people talked about black people and the way they were treated by the government, from what those white women with black bands over their shoulders were doing standing where a white government man was going to pass, I said to myself I said, This woman, *hai*, I do not know, she seems to think very much of us black people. But why was she so sad?

Kate came back home to stay after this. She still played the big gramophone loud-loud-loud and twisted her body at her waist until I thought it was going to break. Then I saw a young white man come often to see her. I watched them through the opening near the hinges of the door between the kitchen and the sitting room where they sat. I saw them kiss each other for a long long time. I saw him lift up Kate's dress and her white-white legs begin to tremble, and — oh I am afraid to say more, my heart was beating hard. She called him Jim. I thought it was funny because white people in the shops call black men Jim.

Kate had begun to play with Jim when I met a boy who

loved me and I loved. He was much stronger than the one I sent away and I loved him more, much more. The face of the doctor came to my mind often, but it did not hurt me so any more. I stopped looking at Kate and her Jim through openings. We spoke to each other, Kate and I, almost as freely as before but not quite. She and her mother were friends again.

Hello, Karabo, I heard Chimane call me one morning as I was starching my apron. I answered. I went to the line to hang it. I saw she was standing at the fence, so I knew she had something to tell me. I went to her.

Hello!

Hello, Chimane!

O kae?

Ke teng. Wena?

At that moment a woman came through the back door of the house where Chimane was working.

I have not seen that one before, I say, pointing with my head.

Chimane looked back, Oh, that one. *Hei*, daughter of the people, *hei*, have you not seen miracles? You know this is Madam's mother-in-law as you see her there. Did I never tell you about her?

White people, nonsense. You know what? That poor woman is here now for two days. She has to cook for herself and I cook for the family.

On the same stove?

Yes, she comes after me when I have finished.

She had her own food to cook?

Yes, Karabo. White people have no heart, no sense.

What will eat them up if they share their food?

Ask me, just ask me. God! She clapped her hands to show

that only God knew, and it was his business not ours.

Chimane asks me she says, Have you heard from home?

I tell her I say, Oh daughter of the people, more and more deaths. Something is finishing the people at home. My mother has written. She says they are all right, my father too and my sisters except for the people who have died. Malebo, the one who lived alone in the house I showed you last year, a white house, he is gone. Then teacher Sedimo. He was very thin and looked sick all the time. He taught my sisters not me. His mother-in-law you remember I told you died last year — no, the year before. Mother says also there is a woman she does not think I remember because I last saw her when I was a small girl she passed away in Zeerust she was my mother's greatest friend when they were girls. She would have gone to her burial if it was not because she has swollen feet.

How are the feet?

She says they are still giving her trouble. I ask Chimane, How are your people at Nokaneng? They have not written?

She shook her head.

I could see from her eyes that her mind was on another thing and not her people at that moment.

Wait for me Chimane eh, forgive me, I have scones in the oven, eh! I will take them out and come back, eh!

When I came back to her Chimane was wiping her eyes. They were wet.

Karabo, you know what?

E-e. I shook my head.

I am heavy with child.

Hau!

There was a moment of silence.

Who is it, Chimane?

Timi. He came back only to give me this.

But he loves you. What does he say have you told him?

I told him yesterday. We met in town.

I remembered I had not seen her at the Black Crow.

Are you sure, Chimane? You have missed a month?

She nodded her head.

Timi himself — he did not use the thing?

I only saw after he finished, that he had not.

Why? What does he say?

He tells me he says, I should not worry I can be his wife.

Timi is a good boy, Chimane. How many of these boys with town ways who know too much will even say, Yes it is my child?

Hai, Karabo, you are telling me other things now. Do you not see that I have not worked long enough for my people? If I marry now who will look after them when I am the only child?

Hm. I hear your words. It is true. I tried to think of something to say.

Then I say, You can talk it over with Timi. You can go home and when the child is born you look after it for three months and when you are married you come to town to work and can put your money together to help the old people while they are looking after the child.

What shall we be eating all the time I am at home? It is not like those days gone past when we had land and our mother could go to the fields until the child was ready to arrive.

The light goes out in my mind and I cannot think of the right answer. How many times have I feared the same thing! Luck and the mercy of the gods that is all I live by. That is all we live by — all of us.

Listen, Karabo. I must be going to make tea for Madam. It will soon strike half-past ten.

I went back to the house. As Madam was not in yet, I threw myself on the divan in the sitting-room. Malan came sniffing at my legs. I put my foot under its fat belly and shoved it up and away from me so that it cried *tjunk — tjunk — tjunk* as it went out. I say to it I say, Go and tell your brother what I have done to you and tell him to try it and see what I will do. Tell your grandmother when she comes home too.

When I lifted my eyes he was standing in the kitchen door, Dick. He says to me he says, *Hau!* Now you have also begun to speak to dogs!

I did not reply. I just looked at him, his mouth ever stretched out like the mouth of a bag, and I passed to my room.

I sat on my bed and looked at my face in the mirror. Since the morning I had been feeling as if a black cloud were hanging over me, pressing on my head and shoulders. I do not know how long I sat there. Then I smelled Madam. What was it? Where was she? After a few moments I knew what it was. My perfume and scent. I used the same cosmetics as Mrs Plum's. I should have been used to it by now. But this morning — why did I smell Mrs Plum like this? Then, without knowing why, I asked myself I said, Why have I been using the same cosmetics as Madam? I wanted to throw them all out. I stopped. And then I took all the things and threw them into the dustbin. I was going to buy other kinds on Thursday; finished!

I could not sit down. I went out and into the white people's house. I walked through and the smell of the house made me sick and seemed to fill up my throat. I went to the bathroom without knowing why. It was full of the smell of Madam. Dick was cleaning the bath. I stood at the door and looked at him cleaning the dirt out of the bath, dirt from Madam's body. *Sies!* I said aloud. To myself I said, Why cannot people wash the dirt of their own bodies out of the bath? Before Dick knew I was near I went out. *Ag,* I said again to myself, why should I think about it now when I have been doing their washing for so long and cleaned the bath many times when Dick was ill? I had held worse things from her body times without number . . .

I went out and stood midway between the house and my room, looking into the next yard. The three-legged grey cat next door came to the fence and our eyes met. I do not know how long we stood like that looking at each other. I was thinking, Why don't you go and look at your grandmother like that, when it turned away and mewed hopping on the three legs. Just like someone who feels pity for you.

In my room I looked into the mirror on the chest of drawers. I thought, is this Karabo this?

Thursday came, and the afternoon off. At the Black Crow I did not see Chimane. I wondered about her. In the evening I found a note under my door. It told me if Chimane was not back that evening I should know that she was at 660 3rd Avenue, Alexandra Township. I was not to tell the white people.

I asked Dick if he could not go to Alexandra with me after I had washed the dishes. At first he was unwilling. But I said to him I said, Chimane will not believe that you refused to come with me when she sees me alone. He agreed.

On the bus Dick told me much about his younger sister

whom he was helping with money to stay at school until she finished, so that she could become a nurse and a midwife. He was very fond of her, as far as I could find out. He said he prayed always that he should not lose his job, as he had done many times before, after staying a few weeks only at each job; because of this he had to borrow money from people to pay his sister's school fees, to buy her clothes and books. He spoke of her as if she were his sweetheart. She was clever at school, pretty (she was this in the photo Dick had shown me before). She was in Orlando Township. She looked after his old people, although she was only thirteen years of age. He said to me he said, Today I still owe many people because I keep losing my job. You must try to stay with Mrs Plum, I said.

I cannot say that I had all my mind on what Dick was telling me. I was thinking of Chimane: what could she be doing? Why that note?

We found her in bed. In that terrible township where night and day are full of knives and bicycle chains and guns and the barking of hungry dogs and of people in trouble. I held my heart in my hands. She was in pain and her face, even in the candlelight, was grey. She turned her eyes on me. A fat woman was sitting in a chair. One arm rested on the other and held her chin in its palm. She had hardly opened the door for us after we had shouted our names when she was on her bench again as if there was nothing else to do.

She snorted, as if to let us know that she was going to speak. She said, There is your friend. There she is my own-own niece who comes from the womb of my sister, my sister who was make to spit out my mother's breast to give way for me. Why does she go and do such an evil thing. *Ao!*

You young girls of today you do not know children die so fast these days that you have to thank God for sowing a seed in your womb to grow into a child. If she had let the child be born I should have looked after it or my sister would have been so happy to hold a grandchild on her lap, but what does it help? She has allowed a worm to cut the roots, I don't know.

Then I saw that Chimane's aunt was crying. Not once did she mention her niece by her name, so sore her heart must have been. Chimane only moaned.

Her aunt continued to talk, as if she was never going to stop for breath, until her voice seemed to move behind me, not one of the things I was thinking: trying to remember signs, however small, that could tell me more about this moment in a dim little room in a cruel township without street lights, near Chimane. Then I remembered the three-legged cat, its grey-green eyes, its *miau*. What was this shadow that seemed to walk about us but was not coming right in front of us?

I thanked the gods when Chimane came to work at the end of the week. She still looked weak, but that shadow was no longer there. I wondered Chimane had never told me about her aunt before. Even now I did not ask her.

I told her I told her white people that she was ill and had been fetched to Nokaneng by a brother. They would never try to find out. They seldom did, these people. Give them any lie, and it will do. For they seldom believe you whatever you say. And how can a black person work for white people and be afraid to tell them lies. They are always asking the questions, you are always the one to give the answers.

Chimane told me all about it. She had gone to a woman

who did these things. Her way was to hold a sharp needle, cover the point with the finger, and guide it into the womb. She then fumbled in the womb until she found the egg and then pierced it. She gave you something to ease the bleeding. But the pain, spirit of our forefathers!

Mrs Plum and Kate were talking about dogs one evening at dinner. Every time I brought something to table I tried to catch their words. Kate seemed to find it funny, because she laughed aloud. There was a word I could not hear well which began with *sem-*: whatever it was, it was to be for dogs. This I understood by putting a few words together. Mrs Plum said it was something that was common in the big cities of America, like New York. It was also something Mrs Plum wanted and Kate laughed at the thought. Then later I was to hear that Monty and Malan could be sure of a nice burial.

Chimane's voice came up to me in my room the next morning, across the fence. When I come out she tells me she says *Hei* child of my father, here is something to tickle your ears. You know what? What? I say. She says, These white people can do things that make the gods angry. More godless people I have not seen. The madam of our house says the people of Greenside want to buy ground where they can bury their dogs. I heard them talk about it in the sitting room when I was giving them coffee last night. *Hei*, people, let our forefathers come and save us!

Yes, I say, I also heard the madam of our house talk about it with her daughter. I just heard it in pieces. By my mother, one day these dogs will sit at table and use knife and fork. These things are to be treated like people now, like children who are never going to grow up.

Chimane sighed and she says, *Hela batho*, why do they

not give me some of that money they will spend on the ground and on the gravestones to buy stockings! I have nothing to put on, by my mother.

Over her shoulder I saw the cat with three legs. I pointed with my head. When Chimane looked back and saw it she said, *Hm*, even *they* live like kings. The mother-in-law found it on a chair and the madam said the woman should not drive it away. And there was no other chair, so the woman went to her room.

Hela!

I was going to leave when I remembered what I wanted to tell Chimane. It was that five of us had collected £1 each to lend her so that she could pay the woman of Alexandra for having done that thing for her. When Chimane's time came to receive money we collected each month and which we took in turns, she would pay us back. We were ten women and each gave £2 at a time. So one waited ten months to receive £20. Chimane thanked us for helping her.

I went to wake up Mrs Plum as she had asked me. She was sleeping late this morning. I was going to knock at the door when I heard strange noises in the bedroom. What is the matter with Mrs Plum, I asked myself. Should I call her, in case she is ill? No, the noises were not those of a sick person. They were happy noises but like those a person makes in a dream, the voice full of sleep. I bent a little to peep through the keyhole. What is this? I kept asking myself. Mrs Plum! Malan! What is she doing this one? Her arm was round Malan's belly and pressing its back against her stomach at the navel, Mrs Plum's body in a nightdress moving in jerks like someone in fits . . . her leg rising and falling . . . Malan silent like a thing to be owned without any choice it can make to belong to another.

The gods save me, I heard myself saying, the words sounding like wind rushing out of my mouth. So this is what Dick said I would find out for myself!

No one could say where it all started; who talked about it first; whether the police wanted to make a reason for taking people without passes and people living with servants and working in town or not working at all. But the story rushed through Johannesburg that servants were going to poison white people's dogs. Because they were too much work for us: that was the reason. We heard that letters were sent to the newspapers by white people asking the police to watch over the dogs to stop any wicked things. Some said that we the servants were not really bad, we were being made to think of doing these things by evil people in town and in the locations. Others said the police should watch out lest we poison madams and masters because black people did not know right from wrong when they were angry. We were still children at heart, others said. Mrs Plum said that she had also written to the papers.

Then it was the police came down on the suburbs like locusts on a cornfield. There were lines and lines of men who were arrested hour by hour in the day. They liked this very much, the police. Everybody they took, everybody who was working was asked, Where's the poison eh? Where did you hide it? Who told you to poison the dogs eh? If you tell us we'll leave you to go free, you hear? And so many other things.

Dick kept saying, It is wrong this thing they want to do to kill poor dogs. What have these things of God done to be killed for? Is it the dogs that make the laws that give us

pain? People are just mad they do not know what they
want, stupid! But when white policemen spoke to him,
Dick trembled and lost his tongue and the things he
thought. He just shook his head. A few moments after they
had gone through his pockets he still held his arms
stretched out, like the man of straw who frightens away
birds in a field. Only when I hissed and gave him a sign did
he drop his arms. He rushed to a corner of the garden to go
on with his work.

Mrs Plum had put Monty and Malan in the sitting room
next to her. She looked very much worried. She called me.
She asked me she said, Karabo, you think Dick is a boy we
can trust? I did not know how to answer. I did not know
whom she was talking about when she said *we*. Then I said,
I do not know, Madam. You know, she said. I looked at her.
I said, I do not know what Madam thinks. She said she did
not think anything, that was why she asked. I nearly
laughed because she was telling a lie this time and not I.

At another time I should have been angry if she lied to
me, perhaps. She and I often told each other lies, as Kate
and I also did. Like when she came back from jail, after that
day when she turned a hosepipe on two policemen. She
said life had been good in jail. And yet I could see she was
ashamed to have been there. Not like our black people who
are always being put in jail and only look at it as the white
man's evil game. Lilian Ngoyi often told us this, and Mrs
Plum showed me how true those words are. I am sure that
we have kept to each other by lying to each other.

There was something in Mrs Plum's face as she was
speaking which made me fear her and pity her at the same
time. I had seen her when she had come from prison; I had
seen her when she was shouting at Kate and the girl left the

house; now there was this thing about dog poisoning. But never had I seen her face like this before. The eyes, the nostrils, the lips, the teeth seemed to be full of hate, tired, fixed on doing something bad; and yet there was something on that face that told me she wanted me on her side.

Dick is all right Madam, I found myself saying. She took Malan and Monty in her arms and pressed them to herself, running her hands all over their heads. They looked so safe, like a child in a mother's arms.

Mrs Plum said, All right you may go. She said, Do not tell anybody what I have asked about Dick eh?

When I told Dick about it, he seemed worried.

It is nothing, I told him.

I had been thinking before that I did not stand with those who wanted to poison the dogs, Dick said. But the police have come out, I do not care what happens to the dumb things now.

I asked him I said, Would you poison them if you were told by someone to do it?

No. But I do not care, he replied.

The police came again and again. They were having a good holiday, everyone could see that. A day later Mrs Plum told Dick to go because she would not need his work any more.

Dick was almost crying when he left. Is Madam so unsure of me, he asked. I never thought a white person could fear me! And he left.

Chimane shouted from the other yard. She said, *Hei ngoana'rona*, the boers are fire-hot eh!

Mrs Plum said she would hire a man after the trouble was over.

A letter came from my parents in Phokeng. In it they told me my uncle had passed away. He was my mother's brother. The letter also told me of other deaths. They said I would not remember some, I was sure to know the others. There were also names of sick people.

I went to Mrs Plum to ask her if I could go home. She asks she says, When did he die? I answer I say, It is three days, Madam. She says, So that they have buried him? I reply, Yes Madam. Why do you want to go home then? Because my uncle loved me very much Madam. But what are you going to do there? To take my tears and words of grief to his grave and to my aunt, Madam. No you cannot go, Karabo. You are working for me you know? Yes, Madam. I, and not your people pay you. I must go Madam, that is how we do it among my people, Madam. She paused. She walked into the kitchen and came out again. If you want to go, Karabo, you must lose the money for the days you will be away. Lose my pay, Madam? Yes, Karabo.

The next day I went to Mrs Plum and told her I was leaving for Phokeng and was not coming back to her. Could she give me a letter to say that I worked for her. She did, with her lips shut tight. I could feel that something between us was burning like raw chillies. The letter simply said that I had worked for Mrs Plum for three years. Nothing more. The memory of Dick being sent away was still an open sore in my heart.

The night before the day I left, Chimane came to see me in my room. She had her own story to tell me. Timi, her boy-friend, had left her — for good. Why? Because I killed his baby. Had he not agreed that you should do it? No. Did he show he was worried when you told him you were heavy? He was worried, like me as you saw me, Karabo.

Now he says if I kill one I shall eat all his children up when we are married. You think he means what he says? Yes, Karabo. He says his parents would have been very happy to know that the woman he was going to marry can make his seed grow.

Chimane was crying, softly.

I tried to speak to her, to tell her that if Timi left her just like that, he had not wanted to marry her in the first place. But I could not, no, I could not. All I could say was do not cry, my sister, do not cry. I gave her my handkerchief.

Kate came back the morning I was leaving, from somewhere very far I cannot remember where. Her mother took no notice of what Kate said asking her to keep me, and I was not interested either.

One hour later I was on the Railway bus to Phokeng. During the early part of the journey I did not feel anything about the Greenside house I had worked in. I was not really myself, my thoughts dancing between Mrs Plum, my uncle, my parents, and Phokeng, my home. I slept and woke up many times during the bus ride. Right through the ride I seemed to see, sometimes in sleep, sometimes between sleep and waking, a red car passing our bus, then running behind us. Each time I looked out it was not there.

Dreams came and passed. He tells me he says, You have killed my seed I wanted my mother to know you are a woman in whom my seed can grow . . . Before you make the police take you to jail make sure that it is for something big you should go to jail for, otherwise you will come out with a heart and mind that will bleed inside you and poison you . . .

The bus stopped for a short while, which made me wake up.

The Black Crow, the club women . . . *Hei*, listen I lie to the madam of our house and I say I had a telegram from my mother telling me she is very very sick. I show her a telegram my sister sent me as if Mother were writing. So I went home for a nice weekend . . .

The laughter of the women woke me up, just in time for me to stop a line of saliva coming out over my lower lip. The bus was making plenty of dust now as it was running over part of the road they were digging up. I was sure the red car was just behind us, but it was not there when I woke.

Any one of you here who wants to be baptized or has a relative without a church who needs to be can come and see me in the office . . . A round man with a fat tummy and sharp hungry eyes, a smile that goes a long, long way . . .

The bus was going uphill, heavily and noisily.

I kick a white man's dog, me, or throw it there if it has not been told the black people's law . . . This is Mister Monty and this is Mister Malan. Now get up you lazy boys and meet Mister Kate. Hold out your hands and say hello to him . . . Karabo, bring two glasses there . . . Wait a bit — What will you chew boys while Mister Kate and I have a drink? Nothing? Sure?

We were now going nicely on a straight tarred road and the trees rushed back. Mister Kate. What nonsense, I thought.

Look Karabo, Madam's dogs are dead. What? Poison. I killed them. She drove me out of a job did she not? For nothing. Now I want her to feel she drove me out for something. I came back when you were in your room and took the things that poisoned them . . . And you know what? She has buried them in clean pink sheets in the garden. *Ao*, clean clean good sheets. I am going to dig them out and take one sheet do you want the other one? Yes, give me the other one I will send it to my mother . . . *Hei*, Karabo, see here they come. Monty and Malan. The bloody fools they do not want to stay in their hole. Go back you silly fools. Oh you do not want to move eh? Come here, now I am going to throw you in the big pool. No, Dick! No, Dick! No, No! Dick! They cannot speak do not kill things that cannot speak. Madam can speak for them she always does. No! Dick . . .

I woke up with a jump after I had screamed Dick's name, almost hitting the window. My forehead was full of sweat. The red car also shot out of my sleep and was gone. I remembered a friend of ours who told us how she and the garden man had saved two white sheets in which the white master had buried their two dogs. They went to throw the dogs in a dam.

When I told my parents my story Father says to me he says, So long as you are in good health my child, it is good. The worker dies, work does not. There is always work. I know when I was a boy a strong sound body and a good mind were the biggest things in life. Work was always there, and the lazy man could never say there was no work. But today people see work as something bigger than everything else, bigger than health, because of money.

I reply I say, Those days are gone Papa. I must go back to the city after resting a little to look for work. I must look after you. Today people are too poor to be able to help you.

I knew when I left Greenside that I was going to return to Johannesburg to work. Money was little but life was full and it was better than sitting in Phokeng and watching the sun rise and set. So I told Chimane to keep her eyes and ears open for a job.

I had been at Phokeng for one week when a red car arrived. Somebody was sitting in front with the driver, a white woman. At once I knew it to be Mrs Plum. The man sitting beside her was showing her the way, for he pointed towards our house in front of which I was sitting. My heart missed a few beats. Both came out of the car. The white woman said "Thank you" to the man after he had spoken a few words to me.

I did not know what to do and how to look at her as she spoke to me. So I looked at the piece of cloth I was sewing pictures on. There was a tired but soft smile on her face. Then I remembered that she might want to sit. I went inside to fetch a low bench for her. When I remembered it afterwards, the thought came to me that there are things I never think white people can want to do at our homes when they visit for the first time: like sitting, drinking water or entering the house. This is how I thought when the white priest came to see us. One year at Easter Kate drove me home as she was going to the north. In the same way I was at a loss what to do for a few minutes.

Then Mrs Plum says, I have come to ask you to come back to me, Karabo. Would you like to?

I say I do not know, I must think about it first.

She says, Can you think about it today? I can sleep at the town hotel and come back tomorrow morning, and if you want to you can return with me.

I wanted her to say she was sorry to have sent me away, I did not know how to make her say it because I know white people find it too much for them to say sorry to a black person. As she was not saying it, I thought of two things to make it hard for her to get me back and maybe even lose me in the end.

I say, You must ask my father first, I do not know, should I call him?

Mrs Plum says, Yes.

I fetched both father and mother. They greeted her while I brought benches. Then I told them what she wanted.

Father asks Mother and Mother asks Father. Father asks me. I say if they agree, I will think about it and tell her the next day.

Father says, It goes by what you feel my child.

I tell Mrs Plum I say, If you want me to think about it I must know if you will want to put my wages up from £6 because it is too little.

She asks me, How much will you want?

Up by £4.

She looked down for a few moments.

And then I want two weeks at Easter and not just the weekend. I thought if she really wanted me she would want to pay for it. This would also show how sorry she was to lose me.

Mrs Plum says, I can give you one week. You see you already have something like a rest when I am in Durban in the winter.

I tell her I say, I shall think about it.

She left.

The next day she found me packed and ready to return with her. She was very pleased and looked kinder than I had ever known her. And me, I felt sure of myself, more than I had ever done.

Mrs Plum says to me, You will not find Monty and Malan.

Oh?

Yes, they were stolen the day after you left. The police have not found them yet. I think they are dead myself.

I thought of Dick . . . my dream. Could he? And she . . . did this woman come to ask me to return because she had lost two animals she loved?

Mrs Plum says to me she says, You know, I like your people, Karabo, the Africans.

And Dick and me? I wondered.

Renewal Time

Though action rages without, the heart can be tuned to produce unbroken music.

So said Acharya Vinoba Bhave, replaying the Hindu scriptures from the Bhagavad-Gita for his fellow prisoners, out there in India in 1932. This, my people, is my unbroken music. Come around, let's talk. When music travels in the wind, who can stop your ears except yourself? Come on over, let us talk. In years to come, when this will be an undivided house and we'll be done spilling blood and guts, and justice and peace and plenty will be what a decent house should contain, we shall most of us remember the history of these times. Remember maybe also the voices we hear from the whirlwind, the dirges that we make; the songs we hear from faraway lands where our players refuse to hang up their harps, because they daren't forget this lovely bleeding land, lest their tongues cleave to the roof of the mouth, lest the ancestors torment them. If these our songs are not remembered in the years to come, amid prosperity or amid other stresses that demand another language, no matter.

Our social concerns change or shift from time to time; the music of today may not raise any applause tomorrow. The memory of singular bleakness or brightness or brownness of past winters or summers or autumns may teach us nothing in particular for this year. But the seasons link up in our own or inherited consciousness, through the years, decades, centuries. The seasons are the unbroken music of our communal experience.

"If you must measure time into seasons, let each season encircle all the other seasons, and let today embrace the past with remembrance, the future with longing." So said Kahlil Gibran. We can remember, whether *we* lived through the seasons or not, the rituals of initiation, of planting, of harvesting — the unbroken celebration of life and death, of triumph or defeat, of heroism and love. They merge with or become seasons of the mind and heart. Here they are immortalized.

And so mine is only one kind of music in the orchestration of our time, which latter is only one segment of time in the cumulative, continuing poetry of our people.

We dreamed once of a house undivided: we began consciously to dream of it when our African pioneers formed a national movement in 1912. And I use "dreamed" not to refer to a "fancy" or a toying with an idea. Those pioneers were an enlightened leadership, and could use only the conventional methods of pleading. We all know the excruciating penalty their successors paid in the Sixties for daring to push further the ideal of an undivided house, an ideal born of an ancient humanism. And now we sing on two sides of a wall, simulating a formidable deafness. We peep through chinks and swinging doors and glass windows to see each other across the barriers. And in broad daylight those who tower over us and their own gods themselves put on dark goggles and say what they see is not real. Flashes, silhouettes, profiles are all we are prepared to see. Why, why?

After we were hurt, after our humanism met with an

uncompromisingly cruel rebuff, we thought we could withdraw, take cover in our own blackness. This time consciously. Unlike hitherto when we took our blackness for granted. Because we had never been made to forget we are black. "Never to forget" had to give way to "always to remember". And then when the people began "always to remember" they had to pay the penalty all over again. Because it was interpreted as "always remember the other man is white". Why, why?

We keep on talking across the wall, singing our different songs, beating our different drums. And yet the artist, always the spearpoint of a people's sensitivity, cannot but feel and express the paradoxes, the ironies, the stupidities, the follies, the resilience, the fortitude, the fears, the ignorance, the tenderness, the hypocrisies, the yearnings, all these deep-deep down, seeping through between our ghettoes white and black, deep down under the foundation of this wall. He can penetrate the social scene in which a people kick about and yell in the attempt to bust the links and disengage from history, because they are entangled with those they deem inferior. The artist pauses, wonders how it must be for anyone to invest all his money, all his time and strength, all his life, in the struggle to live outside of history. If the artist tries to ignore all these realities, it could be because he/she is a prisoner of tribal taboos and other superstitions. Or else he/she is not all there. And we know that in our case, the system was forced upon us. We paid too dearly for our humanism, oh so dearly. Are we going to be made to pay for consolidating our humanism for our separate areas? Once more? May the ancestors cover our naked bodies!

The seepage under the foundation of the wall is but the

southern expression of the entangled destinies of black and white. Since the Portuguese touched the coast of Africa, west and later east, the histories of Europe and Africa have been intertwined, flowing into each other. Wherever walls were erected by the race-conscious Europeans, the water could only sink into the ground in order to flow. Because something's *got* to flow, *something* has got to flow, wherever two persons find each other face to face day after day. You might lay concrete on your side of the wall. Unless you have the means and skill to pave all the fragmented land on his side of the wall, the water from his side must take to subterranean channels and undermine your foundation.

And so we find ourselves in part expressing African thoughts, an African sensibility, in Bantu languages, in English and a few of us in Afrikaans. Fashionable phrases like "protest literature", "addressing white people", "addressing blacks" can be too simplistic. Especially as our literary media are separate. Right there the readership is split down the middle. Africans are exposed to English literature by whites as well as to their own, whites are excluded from African literature.

Which way now, which way? Any wonder that whites feature less and less in African writing at home? Unimportant? No. Maybe simply irrelevant to the black man's understanding of himself, another rejection of the seepage, the flow, down there, underground. A reaction to rejection. But the unbroken music will go on. Though the world outside rages, though the winds whip and lash around, the heart can be tuned.

Come on over . . . let us talk.

Some years to come, when the house will no longer be

divided, we may chat about these times of pain.

And the season of creations will encircle the season of harvesting which will embrace the season of death which will encircle the season of waiting and enduring, spinning out the unbroken song of a people.

The poem, the tale, the play, the direct prose statement of social man all make up the unbroken song. *None of its notes is final*, says Tagore, *yet each reflects the infinite.* By infinite I understand the continuity of the imagination, its perpetual renewal. Toni Cade Bambara, the Afro-American fiction writer, tells us that literature should make revolution irresistible. By revolution I understand renewal. We must come to this song of powerful, memorable, beautiful words for renewal. To help us get our minds and our hearts together. That's how it goes for the rest of the world. In each community the renewal has a cultural purpose, its own.

African Titles from Readers International

Uanhenga Xitu

THE WORLD OF 'MESTRE' TAMODA
£4.95/US$8.95 paperback   £9.95/US$16.95 hardback

The archetypal bush lawyer, mock rhetorician and speechifier Tamoda was conceived in an Angolan colonial prison, but his continuing adventures go beyond the absurdities of white rule to encompass the split between rural and urban life, the rapidly deteriorating African landscape, and the fleeting vision of a possible non-racial society, freed from southern Africa's burden of racial division and violence.

"There is something of him in all of us...like those mimic-men who had no underpants but made sure they wore good-quality trousers." Antônio Jacinto, 1986 NOMA prizewinner.

"Xitu's insights into village life, and the world of pre-independent urban Angola, are both acute and valuable." Caryl Phillips in *The Guardian*

Henri Lopes

THE LAUGHING CRY
£4.95/US$8.95 paperback   £8.95/US$16.95 hardback

An irresistible cock and bull story with the ring of truth. To the sound of military marches over the State Radio, into the Presidential Palace steps Marshal Hannibal-Ideloy Bwakamabé Na Sakkadé, familiarly known as "Daddy," Chief of State, President of the Patriotic Council of National Resurrection, and Recreative Father of his country. Noted Congolese writer Henri Lopes has created the supreme African dictator — a brilliant, ferocious burlesque. The adventures of "Daddy" in the bush, the bar and the bed are a devastating, comic portrait of African power politics today.

"Lopes has captured the truth about Africa." *International Herald Tribune*

"Lopes' book is satirical, tender, bawdy, savage, and filled with love and hope." *Washington Post*

"An Africa that vies with Céline...a beautiful book that will be talked about for a long time." *Nouvel Observateur* (Paris)

African Titles from Readers International

Ahmed Essop

HAJJI MUSA AND THE HINDU FIRE-WALKER
£4.95/US$8.95 paperback   £9.95/US$16.95 hardback

South Africa's Indian community is one of many caught up in the restrictions of *apartheid*. Ahmed Essop's novella and stories give this rich and culturally diverse group its literary voice. Says Lionel Abrahams: "Ahmed Essop is a natural master of the story-teller's art with a fine feeling for situation, character and atmosphere. Though never evasive where the harsh social realities of his chosen scene are concerned, his writing is gentle and balanced in spirit, humor and compassion bringing various levels of comedy and tragedy into his scope. This emotional richness, as well as the vivacious variety of his scene, is reminiscent of V.S.Naipaul."

Es'kia Mphahlele

RENEWAL TIME
£4.95/US$8.95 paperback   £9.95/US$16.95 hardback

This collection marks the odyssey and return of Es'kia Mphahlele to his native South Africa. The range and talent of this great writer, author of the 60's classic *Down Second Avenue*, is demonstrated in these stories from the long period of his exile, plus new impressions of his recent return home to live and teach in the face of today's growing turmoil.

African Titles from Readers International

Njabulo Ndebele

FOOLS AND OTHER STORIES
£4.95/US$8.95 paperback   £8.95/US$14.95 hardback

In these powerful yet delicate narratives, winner of the NOMA
African literature prize, Njabulo Ndebele evokes township life
with humour and subtlety. Ndebele rejects the image of black
South Africans as a "passive people whose only reason for
existing is to receive the sympathy of the world... The
mechanisms of survival and resistance we have devised are many
and far from simple." Instead, he focuses on the complexity
and fierce energy that complicates their lives. The title story
Fools explores the confrontation between two township men of
different generations and the women who bind their lives.
Zamani, a disgraced, middle-aged school teacher meets Zani,
an angry young activist, and an intense relationship of conflict
and growing understanding develops between them.

"For formal elegance and originality, *Fools and Other Stories*
surpasses anything else I've encountered in South African fiction, such excellent works as *Burger's Daughter* and *Life and
Times of Michael K* included." *Village Voice*

"Everything in this book demonstrates splendidly that as a
writer Mr Ndebele has chosen to make his own version of what
Nadine Gordimer called 'the essential gesture'...and he con-
vinces us of the genuineness of his vision in everything he
writes." *New York Times Book Review*

"These begin where the post-Soweto writing gets stuck; they
move on from *apartheid.*" *The Nation*

READ THE WORLD—Books from Readers International

Nicaragua	**To Bury Our Fathers**	Sergio Ramírez	£5.95/US$8.95
Nicaragua	**Stories**	Sergio Ramírez	£3.95/US$7.95
Chile	**I Dreamt the Snow Was Burning**	Antonio Skármeta	£4.95/US$7.95
Brazil	**The Land**	Antônio Torres	£3.95/US$7.95
Argentina	**Mothers and Shadows**	Marta Traba	£3.95/US$7.95
Argentina	**A Funny Dirty Little War**	Osvaldo Soriano	£3.95/US$6.95
Uruguay	**El Infierno**	C. Martínez Moreno	£4.95/US$8.95
Haiti	**Cathedral of the August Heat**	Pierre Clitandre	£4.95/US$8.95
Congo	**The Laughing Cry**	Henri Lopes	£4.95/US$8.95
Angola	**The World of 'Mestre' Tamoda**	Uanhenga Xitu	£4.95/US$8.95
S. Africa	**Fools and Other Stories**	Njabulo Ndebele	USA only $8.95
S. Africa	**Renewal Time**	Es'kia Mphahlele	£4.95/US$8.95
S. Africa	**Hajji Musa and the Hindu Fire-Walker**	Ahmed Essop	£4.95/US$8.95
Iran	**The Ayatollah and I**	Hadi Khorsandi	£3.95/US$7.95
Philippines	**Awaiting Trespass**	Linda Ty-Casper	£3.95/US$7.95
Philippines	**Wings of Stone**	Linda Ty-Casper	£4.95/US$8.95
Japan	**Fire from the Ashes**	ed. Kenzaburō Ōe	£3.50 UK only
China	**The Gourmet**	Lu Wenfu	£4.95/US$8.95
India	**The World Elsewhere**	Nirmal Verma	hbk only £9.95/US$16.95
Poland	**Poland Under Black Light**	Janusz Anderman	£3.95/US$6.95
Poland	**The Edge of the World**	Janusz Anderman	£3.95/US$7.95
Czech.	**My Merry Mornings**	Ivan Klíma	£4.95/US$7.95
Czech.	**A Cup of Coffee with My Interrogator**	Ludvík Vaculík	£3.95/US$7.95
E. Germany	**Flight of Ashes**	Monika Maron	£4.95/US$8.95
E. Germany	**The Defector**	Monika Maron	£4.95/US$8.95
USSR	**The Queue**	Vladimir Sorokin	£4.95/US$8.95

Order through your local bookshop, or direct from the publisher. Most titles also available in hardcover. *How to order:* Send your name, address, order and payment to

RI, 8 Strathray Gardens, London NW3 4NY, UK
or **RI**, P.O. Box 959, Columbia, LA 71418, USA

Please enclose payment to the value of the cover price plus 10% of the total amount for postage and packing. (Canadians add 20% to US prices.)